CURIOUSLY ENCHANTED

WITCHES OF HAWTHORNE GROVE BOOK 2

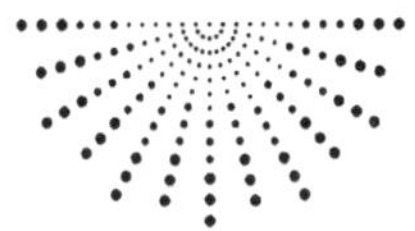

LEIGHANN DOBBS   EMELY CHASE   ANNIE DOBBS

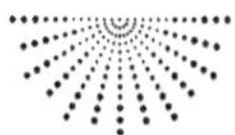

Samuel Ethan Huntingdon III stood in the middle of his mostly bare, eleven hundred and some odd square feet of workshop, both hands stuffed in the pockets of his worn jeans while he watched his newly engaged best friend, Jordan Parker, carefully disassemble the antique *chiffonier* he'd purchased at an estate sale a while back.

"You're going to need to replace some of the hardware." Jordan handed him a door and then the hardware —a pair of ruined iron hinges and what was left of the once intricately crafted wooden pull handle he'd just removed. "You might be able to find these at Seville's. If not, I can check with a few people in Center, but I'd stop in at Seville's first."

Seville's was actually *Seville's Antiques and Collectibles*— a battered, run-down, miserable looking little shop on the opposite edge of town that just happened to be the only genuine antique store in Hawthorne Grove. The place was managed by three sisters who'd lived in the area since way before Sam. He'd only moved into the small town a handful years ago. Jordan had found an antique letter box there a month or so ago, shortly after he'd come to Hawthorne Grove—one he claimed was instrumental in getting him an introduction to his soon to be wife—and Kaylee Dean, his fiance, said the same thing about a snow globe she'd purchased there.

"Great idea," Sam teased. "Maybe I'll run into my future wife while I'm there and we can get started building a replica antique cradle when we finish the restoration of this old thing."

"Go ahead and laugh, old man. Your turn's coming." Jordan shot back, but his reply was muffled because he was leaning head and shoulders inside the cabinet, thumping and fumbling around with something inside.

Shelves, most likely, Sam thought, until the one door that was still attached swung back and Jordan emerged, holding what looked like an old quilt rack—at least that's what Sam thought it was. That was what his Grandmother had always called the things she kept near the foot of every bed in her house, anyway.

This one was a little bit plain. It was bare and dusty and a little beat up, but with some wax and polish and some good old TLC, Sam knew it would be as good as new. He reached out to take it to set it aside for now but Jordan was too busy inspecting the thing to hand it over.

"What in the world? Looks like a hand-made saw

horse or something," Jordan said, eyeing the piece quizzically. "No, I don't think so, now that I give it a closer look. It's too detailed for that but I've never seen anything like it before. You got any ideas, Sammy?"

"It's a quilt rack," he informed Jordan. He was feeling more than a little proud to be able to claim some knowledge—in this area at least. "Grandma used to have one of these in every bedroom."

Each one always seemed to be holding a different variety of hand-sewn quilts, too, as he recalled, all lovingly stitched by his grandmother and sometimes, a few of her friends. The smell of springtime and sunshine seemed to have been infused into them, too, now that he thought about it. Grandma never had embraced the idea of electric dryers. She hung her quilts outdoors on the clothesline Grandpa had stretched for her until the day she'd died and the scent of her quilts, one of linens freshly taken in off the line, was one Sam thought he'd never forget. He'd been snuggling into the things since he was a toddler.

Shaking free of an unexpected wave of nostalgia, he glanced up and caught Jordan still eyeing the wooden rack skeptically and tried to explain. "A *quilt* rack, Jordan. You know? A place where you store your extra quilts when they're not being used every night but it's still too cool out to stuff them away into the back of the linen closet for summer storage?"

He reached over to take the piece from his friend and set it carefully to one side. "I remember coming in late, sneaking up the back stairs before Grandma passed away. She would catch me every time. She'd give me a pat, feel my cheeks, worry over how chilled I was, and tell me there were plenty of extra quilts by the bed if I needed them. All I had to do was pick one and snuggle in."

"Grandma Ellie." Jordan nodded. "She was a great lady, Sam. I know you miss her."

Sam nodded. "She and Grandpa were the only constants in my life. Dad was always out in his rig on yet another cross-country run, but the only running Grandma ever did was to the grocery store on Wednesdays. Remember that? I used to think the only reason she went there was to pick up ingredients to make her famous cookies. "

Jordan straightened, moving so he could lean one hip against the wardrobe, a smile of fond reminiscence on his lips. He chuckled. "Double fudge chocolate chip. How could I forget?"

Sam's laughter joined Jordan's but then he glanced toward the front of the shop when Kaylee Dean, Jordan's fiance, poked her head around the workshop door. "Jordan? Did Sam forget Lindsay's supposed to stop by the coffee shop today, or have you two decided to skip the meeting and just play in here all day instead?"

Lindsay Vale, the owner of *Vale's Vintage Interiors* and a long-time friend of Kaylee's older sister, Jo Dean Leavy, was coming in to talk with Sam about renovating the interior of the coffee shop. Her beautiful vintage makeovers had landed her multiple interviews and a number of choice features in a few high profile interior design magazines and these days her calendar was solidly booked with clients. But lucky for Sam, Lindsay had a passion for his place and had been itching to talk to him about it for a while now. Jo said she'd practically jumped up and down when she'd got the call from Sam to stop by for a consultation.

Jordan handed over the hardware he'd removed from the *chiffonier* and hurried across the shop to greet Kaylee with a warm kiss while Sam looked wryly on. "We were just about to head out, Kaylee. Now that you're here, you can help us wrangle Sarge out of Sammy's forty acre field out back."

Kaylee laughed. The "field" in question was really just a huge back yard Sam had recently fenced in where his new Husky pup, Jabez, was allowed to roam free. "Sarge loves it when you bring him for a visit now. I think he likes playing protector."

It only took a minute for Jordan and Kaylee to collect the Golden Retriever Jordan had adopted from the animal shelter where Kaylee worked a few months ago from Sam's back yard and then Sam walked with them to Jordan's pick-up.

"I'll meet you two at the coffee shop," he promised Kaylee. "Jordan says I should stop by Seville's to look for replacement hardware for the *chiffonier* and since it's on the way, I think I'll stop in." He offered a casual shrug. "If the sisters don't have what I need, maybe you can ask around in Center this afternoon when you and Jordan go up to look at wedding dresses?"

Kaylee hopped up onto the passenger side seat, a grin slowly spreading across her lips. "Oh, I think the Seville's will have exactly what you need, Sammy. Don't rush. If Lindsay shows up at the One Shot before you, Jordan and I will keep her entertained until you get there. Take your time!"

Sam waved goodbye to his friends and went to the house to collect his keys and a jacket, shaking his head all the while at Kaylee's not so subtle insinuation. How could the Seville sisters possibly know what he needed in his life when he didn't have a clue himself?

THE SOFT SOUND of musical bells ringing over the door of the antique shop was accompanied by an almost electrical hum of awareness that brought Emma Riley's head springing up, but only long enough for her to peek inquisitively through her lashes and over the rim of her glasses to see who had come inside.

A tallish man with hair the color of wet sand and a contagious friendly smile walked into the showroom, surprise clearly evident on his face at how different the interior of the small antique shop was in comparison with the almost frighteningly debilitated look of the exterior.

Hiding a smile of her own, Emma quickly ducked her

head back down before he could make eye contact, forcing herself to focus once again on the display of antique puzzles in front of her instead of checking him out.

As a Freelance Research Specialist, her job often brought her into contact with all sorts of rare, artful things, but her latest client—a fiction writer—needed some information about antique puzzles and that was why she had driven down here this morning—to see what she could find, if anything, at Seville's.

Lindsay Vale, her roommate from college and probably what most people would call a best friend, had suggested this particular shop. Lindsay was an interior decorator and she frequently hung out in antique shops or at estate sales looking for the perfect pieces with which to transform the bland, boring interiors of her clientele.

Lindsay had warned her about the fallacy of Seville's battered exterior, promising sheer magic awaited her beyond the ramshackle appearance and half-rotted wooden doors. Emma hadn't been so certain when she'd gotten her first look at the place. Once inside, however, she'd found herself enchanted by the beautiful selections on offer.

Right now, she was having a difficult time making up her mind over which of the puzzles waiting with infinite patience in front of her she should buy. Even though she hadn't come in this morning with the intent to actually purchase a puzzle, now that she was here, looking directly at them instead of viewing them from a set of badly shot photographs on the Internet, she couldn't seem to will herself to resist.

One puzzle in particular, made from an especially warm hardwood with a slightly worn image of a charming Victorian couple on front, pulled at her. She knew she'd probably settle on it in the end, but right now, she was enjoying the momentary back and forth debate in her mind of trying to decide between it and another which sported an ancient world map—which she also loved—but that one seemed far less sophisticated in regard to the cut of the individual pieces.

"Good morning! Can we help you, sir?" came the lilting voice of the woman who had settled behind the counter a few moments before, right after she'd carefully lain out the most interesting quilt Emma had ever seen. Made up of black and white squares, each one sewn together in a lovely pattern she knew probably had a name though she hadn't a clue what it might be, Emma figured the only reason she found the antique coverlet intriguing was because it was so simple. The piece was crisp. Practical. Useful. A bit like herself, she supposed. Maybe that was why the thing kept drawing her eye?

"It is lovely, isn't it?" The woman behind the counter ran her hand over the material in a gentle sweep, caressing the fabric as if it were something precious and rare. "The lady we acquired it from said it had been in her family for at least six generations, and look—not a stitch out of place after all this time."

"My grandmother made one like this once, only she used bits of multicolored fabric where this one has solids. Interesting that this piece was done in simple black and white," the man who had come in earlier replied. His voice moved over her slowly; like a ray of sunshine stepping boldly from behind the shadows of a cloud, it warmed her.

Blushing at the realization, Emma cast a quick, surreptitious gaze in his direction and sucked in a breath of surprise. She had somehow managed to gravitate over to the counter without the slightest awareness of having done so and was now standing right beside him—so close she could feel the heat emanating from his body. No wonder she imagined his voice was warming her like the sun!

Flustered now, she glanced down at the quilt they'd been discussing. The sight of his large, tanned hand resting firmly atop the cloth started a flutter in her ribcage and her gaze jerked upward once more. It clashed with his and held, refusing to break away.

"The simplicity of it is what makes it so special," Emma said, responding in a voice gone breathless, and to her surprise, he wholeheartedly agreed.

"I'll take it," he said, glancing up at the proprietress. "Along with four sets of each of these if you have them." He held out his other hand to show the woman what he needed before handing over the hinges, and Emma, now freed from the intensity of his gaze, was suddenly galvanized into action.

"Oh, no. You can't! I—It's—" Emma laid the puzzle box she didn't remember picking up on the counter beside the quilt and turned an imploring gaze on the woman behind it as her fingers found and slid like a caress over the warm cloth. "I—I'd already decided to purchase it you see," she fibbed, stuttering out an explanation while her eyes silently willed the shopkeeper to go along before she said, "Um, yes, and I'll take the puzzle, too."

Guilt over her fib instantly plaguing her, Emma tilted her head upward by tiny degrees until her eyes met the doubtful suspicion in his—and she could feel the cloth beneath her fingertips changing, firming, expanding until it seemed to have come alive. It now felt as if she were caressing the planes and contours of a slightly stumbled chin. A *male* chin—just like that of the man standing beside her.

Emma snatched her hand away and quickly turned her head to break eye contact with the handsome stranger but not before she noticed the flecks of tawny gold highlighting his eyes go bright, changing the lucent green to a marbled, molten amber.

Flushed with embarrassment, her face heated. He couldn't possibly have known what she was thinking. Could he? Keeping her gaze lowered, she merely nodded her head when the woman behind the counter asked if she wanted the puzzle and quilt wrapped. She could sense movement at her side, but didn't dare look up again. Not while he was still there.

The minute the puzzle and quilt were both wrapped and bagged, Emma hastily signed her name on the check she'd been making out and handed it to the woman, then grabbed up both packages and hurried from the store, head down, her eyes firmly focused on nothing but the path in front of her.

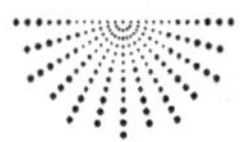

CHAPTER TWO

Mortianna Seville waited until the bells over the door quieted before she swept into the main showroom of the antique shop with a dull gray cardboard box clutched in one hand. The other, she used to motion to Serephina.

"Put it over there," she said, pointing to a cleared stretch of counter space slightly to the left of the register at the checkout area where Esmerelda currently stood. "If it doesn't sell soon, well, at least we will have a lovely decoration to look at while we pass time behind the counter."

The *decoration* in question was a lovely twelve piece, English rose patterned antique coffee set and every one of those pieces were marked with the numbers 214 on the bottom but even if there had been no numbers the sisters would have known precisely who this particular grouping was for: Sam Huntingdon, owner of the popular coffee shop out at the edge of town.

Serephina carefully balanced the tray, wincing when the near-priceless pieces rattled as she transferred the setting to the counter top. She cringed, but Mortianna noticed it was more of a distracted reaction because her attention wasn't really on the heirloom bone china at all. Instead, she had been staring, both brows arched high in questioning demand at Esmerelda.

Mortianna could have walked over and warned her younger sister about the impending furor but instead she simply watched as Serephina gingerly moved each of the pieces of the coffee set into place—straightening here, aligning there until she was satisfied with the arrangement—and all the while continuing and failing in her not so subtle attempts to catch Esmerelda's eye.

Finally, Serephina gave up trying to make eye contact and retreated slowly toward the back of the storeroom again, this time motioning ever so slightly with a quick, jerky little nod of her head in yet another covert attempt to encourage Esmerelda to notice and to follow her.

Esmerelda didn't. In fact, she hadn't done anything except stare at the door since their last customer had left.

Mortianna knew something was wrong. From the not so subtle hints Serephina was giving to Esmerelda's uncharacteristic daze, she had her warning that all was not as it should be. But the pieces of this particular "what-is-going-on-now" puzzle hadn't quite managed to fall together enough to tell her exactly which of Esmerelda's actions had gone south.

Pasting on a smile, she swept over to the counter to greet Sam. "Excuse me. You wanted hardware, right? Hinges, I believe?" She handed him the box. "These come in lots of twenty, so you'll have a few extra if you need them. Will that be all or is there something else we can get for you today?"

Like Esmerelda, she noticed, his eyes were also still focused on the door. He nodded inattentively, then shook his head no as he reached distractedly into his back pocket for his wallet. "How much?"

"Forty-one twenty," Esmerelda finally murmured quietly from behind the counter, sounding very much as if she were lost in thought and miles away. "Do you need a bag?"

"Of course he doesn't need a bag, silly. They are all boxed up already." Mortianna blurted, her words followed by a warm chuckle as she smiled up at Mr. Huntingdon again then sidled around the counter to sit near her sister on one of the stools. "You're Sam, right? From the coffee shop?"

"How did you guess?" Sam asked, then quickly ducked his head to sniff at his person. "Do I smell like coffee beans?"

This time Mortianna's chuckle was low and bordered on what she hoped sounded provocative. "Yes. A sinfully rich Arabian brew, actually."

Leaning forward, she propped her elbow on the

counter and rested her chin in one hand, keeping her attention utterly centered on the man on the other side. "You're doing something new over there, I hear. Renovations?"

"Very soon. Going vintage." Sam shrugged. "I thought it was time to dress the place up a little. You should come in. Have coffee. We serve a wicked mean caramel latte that most of my female customers swear by."

"Oh, I'll bet it's decadent," Mortianna said, following her assessment with a dreamy sigh. "One sip would likely be bliss, but I've got these crazy allergies?"

Grabbing a tissue from beneath the counter, she nodded toward the coffee set. The tissue, she waved up and down in front of Esmerelda before swishing it in an upward arc toward the door to the storeroom where Serephina now paced back and forth in a worried march, but like Serephina's attempts to gain her attention before, the subtlety of her attempted signal was lost on Esmerelda.

Covering her nose with the tissue, Mortianna faked a sneeze, then immediately nodded toward the coffee service again and asked Sam, "Do you think *this* might be a good piece for the new look you're after? Feeny says it once belonged to a Queen so it's probably ancient but it still looks nice."

Sam picked up one of the cups and turned it in his hand. "My grandmother had a set like this when I was a kid. I remember she always kept it on the kitchen table.

Grandpa never touched it but every morning before school—"

His words broke off and he slanted a quick, questioning gaze at her. "Do you have any of those cloth things that go under stuff like this? Grandma, she had these webby, lace-like circles and squares underneath the coffee server and the sugar and cream pots—dollies, or something like that," he explained while making motions with his hands meant to define the 'webby things' he couldn't seem to recall the name of. "And lace-edged napkins. They were the only pieces of what my Grandpa called 'feminine frippery' she ever owned."

"Webbed and lace-like … oh, you mean *doilies*? Yes, we do have doilies," Mortianna assured him. "Exquisite ones. Napkins, too, all edged with the finest Battenberg lace. We also have a table runner. Two actually. White and cream," she said, holding up one of each. "Which do you prefer?"

"I'll go with the cream," he said. "There are six cups so we'd better make it six napkins, too."

Mortianna slid off the stool and pulled a thin stack of wrapping material from beneath the counter. "I'll wrap these while Merry collects the doilies. Do you like puzzles, Mr. Huntingdon?"

His brows rose at the unrelated question. "Not especially, but now that you mention it, I suppose an antique one with one of those Old World scenes on top could add a nice something to the look and feel of the new décor."

"You're right and I agree that it would," Mortianna said with a slow nod. Watching him as carefully as she was, she knew the exact moment he realized her question hadn't been related to the renovations at his coffee shop at all but to the puzzle piece she had seen him covertly filch from their last customer's purchase. His eyelids lowered and his expression suddenly closed.

"I put my card in the box in exchange." He offered the explanation with a shrug. "If she wants the piece back, she will know where to get it."

This time Mortianna's chuckle was less provocative and more the low sound of genuine appreciation for a fine move well played. "I do believe you've an impish humor, Mr. Huntingdon."

Esmerelda returned with the doilies and lace napkins and immediately started placing the delicate pieces of the antique coffee service into a foam-lined box. Mortianna helped, sliding the now wrapped tops to the sugar dish and coffee pot into the side between two layers of protective foam.

"Cunning, but impish," she pointed out with a smile. "Will you trade it for the quilt?"

"That's a great idea, actually!" Sam said, his eyes suddenly alight with a brilliant spark of the impish good humor she had accused him of having. Mortianna thought his slow grin made him look almost boyish. "Do you think she would agree?"

Sliding a snug, triple-reinforced paper top over the box, she moved to the register. "I don't think you'll get the chance to find out, honestly. The lady seemed very shy to me."

"While I, on the other hand, am not," he said, dropping the words she *hadn't* said in a casual and as unconcerned manner as he'd had when taking the puzzle piece from her last customer while she wasn't looking. Another shrug lifted his shoulders. "If she doesn't call or come by the coffee shop soon, I will find a way to get the piece to her."

Mortianna speared him with a doubtful look as she rang up his purchases. "That will be one-hundred and fifty, even. Do I have your word on that, Mr. Huntingdon?"

"Oh, absolutely." Sam handed over his credit card. Three minutes later, he was walking out the door with his hinges and a very high dollar coffee service which had once belonged to royalty.

Inside the store, Mortianna turned to Esmerelda, her eyes gleaming with pleasure. "That man is *fun*! Unlike you," she pooed, giving her sister a quick nudge. "What is up with that face?"

"*This* one?" Esmerelda demanded in an unexpectedly agitated—no, it was a *furious* tone, Mortianna decided— and it sliced out from between tight lips on a face sporting an ever darkening scowl.

"Do you mean this particular look of utter horror and abject misery that's currently written all over my face?" Esmerelda uncharacteristically demanded again, her hand sweeping upward to indicate the face in question--hers. "The one you are witnessing right *freakin'* now?"

With a roll of her eyes at her sister's far too over-played dramatics, Mortianna's brows rose high. "Why, yes! I *do* mean that one! However did you guess?"

Groaning with as much misery as the look on her face held, Esmerelda spun around. "Didn't you notice? It's the expression that sprouted the minute I realized *fun* is the *last* thing we are going to be having any time soon, thanks to my distraction! Like, for the next hundred years or so!"

Casting a pleading look at Serephina, who now stood quietly waiting in the open doorway between the shop and the back room, her arms crossed loosely in front of her and one shoulder propped against the jamb, Esmerelda asked, "I sold the quilt to the wrong woman, didn't I?"

CHAPTER THREE

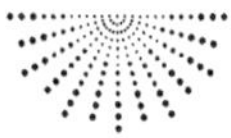

*D*ragged from a deep, drowning kind of sleep —the kind of slumberous stupor you normally had to fight to wake up from—Emma's eyes snapped open.

Disoriented and annoyed at having been snatched from her dream at such an inopportune time, her gaze flicked from wall to door to wall on its journey around the room before she turned her head slowly on the pillow she was clutching to find her fingers still clenched tight, digging into the soft cotton material of the black and white patterned quilt that covered her.

Her cheeks were burning, her pulse racing in reaction to the dream she'd been having.

About *him*.

She gulped in a breath seeking to calm the erratic thrum of her wildly beating heart, but her devious mind had other ideas insisting replaying the last few scenes of the dream over in her head. The dream where the man with the too bold stare from the antique store was just about to kiss her.

For the past three nights in a row, she had dreamed of him.

Three nights!

A man whose name she did not even know!

A *stranger.*

Embarrassed despite the fact she was totally alone in her own bed, in her own apartment, and knowing she was the only one who could possibly ever know what she'd dreamed, Emma's hands flew up to cover her damp, flushed face. How in the world could she have such dreams about a complete stranger?

Yes, he was good looking.

Yes, his voice had had that sultry quality about it that made her insides seem to melt when he spoke.

Yes, she *had* had that strange reaction to him in the antique store a few days ago—but they'd barely spent five minutes together! That should not have been enough contact with the man to make her *dream* about him!

Groaning in annoyance, Emma tossed the quilt and sheet to one side and swung her legs over the side of her bed. Beside her, the covers shook and wiggled; a furry white paw poked its way from beneath the quilt, followed by a pink nose and snowy whiskers. Emma reached over and scooped the cat up, then sat her carefully on the bed. "Sorry, Chloe. I didn't mean to wake you, girl, or to bury you in my blankets but I had *that dream* again."

There was definitely derision in her tone, but if Chloe picked up on it, the feline didn't react. Instead, she sat back on her hind legs and indulged in a long, drawn out yawn before blinking, sleepy-eyed, up at Emma.

Fumbling around with her feet in the semi-darkness of her bedroom for her slippers, Emma glanced at the pale blue glow of numbers lighting the digital clock on her nightstand. 5:48 AM. "Great."

Normally, she slept until eight, but these past few nights had wreaked havoc on her schedule with her dreams waking her at all hours and the lack of sleep left her feeling tired and distracted for the rest of the day. "And grumpy," she grumbled aloud.

Toes now firmly tucked into her slippers, she padded to the bathroom. "Shower first, Chloe, then I'll tell you all about it."

Forty-five minutes later, she had finished her shower, dressed, made coffee, and was fiddling with the seven charms hanging from the silver bracelet she'd discovered clinging to a loose thread on the quilt she'd bought from the antique store when her cell phone rang.

Thrilled for the distraction, she swiped it up off the counter and peered at the screen. *Vale's Vintage Interiors.* She touched the screen to accept the call and put the phone on speaker. "Lindsay, hi! I was just thinking about you!" And she had been. Lindsay loved charm bracelets and Emma had been thinking this one would make a great gift for her.

"Hi yourself! You're up early! But then, I hoped you would be. Listen," Lindsay chirped happily. "Wanna come with me this morning? Say yes and I'll buy you a cup of the finest coffee Hawthorne Grove has to offer."

Glancing at the freshly brewed pot awaiting her on the counter, Emma started to decline, but Lindsay interrupted her refusal before she could utter the words.

"I'm working with a new client. He owns the local coffee shop out there and that place serves some amazing joe. Come on, Emma. You're only going to spend the day staring at your computer again if you don't, right? Don't say no."

Without bothering to remind her long-time friend that *staring at the computer all day* was actually what she did for work, Emma glanced desperately at Chloe as if seeking some sort of feline intervention. A coffee shop was very public and generally filled with lots and lots of people and a people person Emma was not.

Chloe looked up as if she had been intently listening to the entire conversation and was now waiting to see if her mistress would agree to the outing or not. Emma arched a brow in question and Chloe tilted her chin upward, giving a slow shift and flick of her tail before turning her attention back to her bowl, ignoring Emma in favor of her breakfast. Emma narrowed her eyes at the cat but then chuckled. "Looks like Chloe doesn't mind if I leave for a bit, so I guess that's a yes. Should I meet you there, or...?"

"Thank Heaven for Chloe!" Lindsay laughed. "No, don't bother with the car. I'll pick you up at your place in … is half an hour okay?"

If the past few days were any indication, half an hour would not be nearly long enough. Every day it was taking Emma longer and longer to rid her thoughts of the dream, but she agreed anyway. "Oh, and I have something for you. It's a bracelet—a charm one. You're going to love it!"

And love it she did. Lindsay hadn't taken her eyes off the thing once during the entire ride to the coffee shop which Emma spent telling her all about about the disturbing dreams she'd been having.

"So what do *you* think?" Emma asked as she walked beside Lindsay while Lindsay continued to admire the bracelet now hanging beautifully from her wrist. "Am I completely out of it? Dreaming about a total stranger—I mean, it's so odd, isn't it?"

"Huh? Oh. Well, maybe a little, but I wouldn't worry about it," Lindsay brushed off her concern with a shrug. "You spend so much time buried in all that research, Emma, you don't have any left over for yourself. Maybe your dreams are just trying to tell you you need more?"

"More what?" Emma asked. "It's kind of difficult to have more of something you're not currently getting any of, you know."

Once again, Lindsay adjusted the silver charms

dangling from the bracelet on her wrist with a quick flick of her other hand. "Your dreams are just telling you you're up for a bit of a distraction, Emma; a change. A quick little pick-me-up. *Coffee.*"

Emma stared at her. "Coffee? You think the dreams I just described are my subconscious's way of saying I need *coffee*?"

"Yes, that's it," Lindsay said, settling her cream colored cashmere jacket into place before she continued. "Coffee! You definitely need coffee and, well *voila!* Here I am, happy to provide!"

Emma scoffed and shook her head. "Maybe *I'm* not the one who's a little off."

~

SAM RECOGNIZED the woman from the antique shop the second he spied her coming across the lot with Lindsay. Red hair. Glasses. That distracted air about her that seemed more due to a deep internal focus than any outward stimulus. Even from here, where he stood with Gem behind the *barista's* counter, she seemed aloof.

His first reaction was irritation.

After he'd left Seville's, he'd been to six different shops looking for a quilt like the one she'd snatched right out from under him the other day but no one had anything even marginally resembling the one she'd got. He'd missed Lindsay's last appointment because of it— because he'd been so determined to at least find something *close* to the quilt Little Miss Red Hair and Glasses had scooped up before he could open his mouth to make an offer for it.

Not that he had a clue why that particular style of quilt had suddenly become so important to him. All he had known at the time was that it *had* and *she* had robbed him of the chance to own it.

Bottling his annoyance, he wiped the earthenware mug he'd been drying one last time and stepped up to the bar so Lindsay and her friend would be sure to see him when they walked in. He glanced at his watch. One minute after. Late but not late. He grinned.

"It's about time you got here," he teased when Lindsay and her red-haired companion walked inside. "I'd almost decided to call in your competition so I can finally get something done around here!"

"Bite your tongue, Samuel Huntingdon," Lindsay fired back as she slipped out of her coat. "My competition would just bankrupt you and leave you with exactly what you already have. At least you'll get a few genuinely useful tips out of me before *I* hit the road with your life savings."

Sam chuckled, then motioning to the timid lady at her side, he asked, "Who do we have here? Wait, haven't I seen you someplace recently?"

"Sam Huntingdon, Emma Riley," Lindsay said, motioning with one hand from one to the other as she made the introduction. "Emma's a long-time friend and a die-hard coffeeholic, so surely you can imagine my surprise when she told me she'd never been in here before."

She shook her head and tugged at the hems of her layered shirts while her gaze swept around the coffee shop, then, propping her hands on her hips, she glanced back at Sam, brows drawn and eyes narrowed. "Emma lives about twenty minutes away and not once has the aromatic call of your brew lured her here for an early morning cuppa. You're slipping, Huntingdon. What's up with that?"

Lindsay peered at him for a second and then shook her head as if to say, *What a shame*. Sam's brow rose. He stuck out a hand to Emma. "Well, there's a thing I can definitely do something about. Gem! Get Lindsay and her friend a cup, won't you? On the house," he murmured in an aside to Emma when he saw her reach for her purse.

Their eyes met and her cheeks immediately colored. The smile she offered was a tad bit shaky, too, if he wasn't mistaken. Curious, he tilted his head to the side and let his eyes ask the questions his brain told his lips to ignore.

"Thank you," she murmured, ignoring his inquisitive gaze. "And we *have* met before though we weren't introduced. Seville's?"

Sam snapped his fingers as if he had only just recalled where he had seen her before. "That's it! *You're* the lady who was in front of me the other day. You picked up one of those wood-carved puzzle things, right?"

Turning to Lindsay, he explained, "She was in line ahead of me and unfortunately she left before I had a chance to question her about her caffeine habits."

"Mm," Lindsay hummed. "And you no doubt question everyone you meet about those, right?"

"Um, coffee shop? Hello?" He gestured to indicate the shop and grinned. "Of course I do. Would have got around to it with your Emma here eventually, too, but I was distracted by—"

"Her eyes?" Lindsay's eyes were sparkling brightly now with the light of merriment over being allowed to indulge with him in some good-natured teasing. "Of course you were. They *are* the color of deep, rich coffee, after all."

Sam noted the way Emma's breath caught right before her shocked gaze flew up to meet his and he bit back another chuckle. Was it his imagination or had Lindsay just embarrassed her? He couldn't help but notice, though, that what Lindsay said about her eyes was true. They *were* a perfect blend of dark and light, like warm coffee and rich cream, one color swirled into the other until…

Realizing his thoughts had wandered into territory which would be impolite to explore at the moment, Sam cleared his throat and walked back around the end of the bar. "I think it's time we stopped chattering on about your friend as if she weren't here and got down to business. And speaking of business," he said with a nod toward Emma, "You girls are going to *swoon* over my find at the antique store."

"*Swoon?* What an archaic choice of word." Lindsay teased as she moved curiously forward to inspect his find. "I love it!"

There was a rattle, the sound of delicate little cups rocking in their perch on matching saucers, as Sam lifted the coffee service he'd picked up at Seville's from a shelf beneath the bar.

"This," he said, giving the coffee server a quick tap. "This once belonged to *a queen.*"

Lindsay laughed. "A *queen?* Well, anything I could offer you now would certainly pale in comparison," she said, but her hands were already reaching for the lace edged napkins, her eyes busily searching the interior for a place to put everything he'd brought out.

He kept his eyes on Emma, but to Lindsay, Sam said, "You remember Jordan, right? He is restoring a *chiffonier* for me that will serve as the perfect display case for this and we already know we are going to put it right over here at the end of the bar. But now that *you* are here, we can talk about what to do with the rest of the room..."

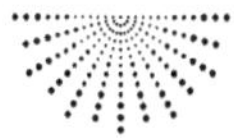

CHAPTER FOUR

*L*indsay had explained to Emma on the drive over how she'd been introduced to Sam a couple years ago so their easy banter was no surprise but with the two of them now fully absorbed in their conversation about changes to be made to the coffee shop and her with nothing productive or even related to add, Emma felt a little out of place.

The barista, Gem, sat two mugs of steaming coffee in front of her and after a quick, sidelong glance at Lindsay to see if she was paying enough attention that she would notice her absence if she moved away, Emma sidled quietly toward the alluring, aromatic call of coffee.

Perched on a stool, she sipped at the frothy brew, her attention drawn to the antique coffee service now seemingly forgotten by coffee shop owner and interior designer alike. Had it really once belonged to a royal family? If so, she wondered, how had it managed to fall into the hands of the Seville sisters? Were the royals long dead?

Those questions only managed to rouse more, awakening the researcher in Emma until her inborn curiosity and a newly birthed wonder over the antique coffee service was fully engaged. Lifting a cup, she peered at the bottom, searching for an inscription. Finding only a small group of numbers and what might be a potter's mark—antlers or possibly crossed swords?—she committed them to memory and carefully replaced it on the tray.

A glance over her shoulder revealed that Lindsay and Sam—whom she now knew was the guy from Seville's—were still in deep, though animated, conversation so she rummaged in her purse for her notebook and pencil and started a quick sketch of the service that she could refer to later.

Time and again while her pencil rapidly skimmed the page her gaze were drawn back to Sam and each time it was, she felt her face heat even more. *Stop it, Emma,* she grouched to herself. *There's no reason for your silly blushes. He doesn't know he's had a starring role in your dreams for the past three nights!*

Glancing down at her notebook during one of her not so rare "argue with myself again" moments, she gasped. To the side of her sketch of the antique coffee service was a nicely rendered drawing of Sam Huntingdon—only she hadn't captured his likeness the way he looked today but the way she had seen him so many times in her dreams. Snapping the notebook shut, she shoved it and her pencil into her purse and forced herself to look away, out the curved bank of windows on the other side of the shop to distract herself.

It didn't help.

Sam's face was reflected in each pane of the glass and despite her fervid self-lectures to the contrary, the knowing look in his eyes said he was well aware of the nature of her thoughts if not the nature of her dreams these past few nights but that he was happy to let her stew in embarrassment over fear of being caught out.

Ridiculous.

Forcing her eyes to study the liquid in her cup, Emma admitted she'd found it a little odd that he remembered the puzzle she'd bought but hadn't said a word about the quilt she'd practically snatched out of his hands. If memory served—and judging by the level of dream detail her recall had been serving up to her since she followed Lindsay into the coffee shop, she was certain it did—he had seriously wanted that quilt. So why hadn't he mentioned it?

Puzzled, she turned on the stool to peer questioningly over her shoulder at him—and found him blatantly staring back. She froze. He *knew*. He knew his attention was disturbing her and she suspected he kept returning it to her on purpose—was it some kind of game with him? Her eyes narrowed and when the corners of his lips kicked up in a responsive little grin, she was sure of it.

But—how could he possibly know what she had dreamed?

He doesn't, you little idiot, the voice inside her head screamed. *But if you don't stop gasping and blushing like a teen-ager every time he looks your way, he is bound to figure out* something's *going on for sure!*

Juvenile, she decided.

Her behavior was bordering on juvenile and there was far too much remembered pain buried in memories of her youth for her to want to revisit them now. She never wanted—or intended—to be *that* girl, ever again.

Straightening on the stool, she pointedly turned her back to him and sipped at her coffee, keeping her eyes focused on her cup and her attention purposely off of Sam while he and Lindsay finished their conversation.

"Put in that call to Rowena," Lindsay said as she and Sam rejoined Emma at the bar. Reaching for her cup, she added, "There's not a lot of foot traffic—or any traffic, for that matter—by her place right now. Her sales are strictly word of mouth. I'm sure she would be delighted by the chance to relocate to a busier location."

"Hmm, not to mention the second floor of a Victorian mansion would fit right in with her image. Nightshades —Hawthorne Grove's only after-hours florist." Sam shook his head. "I still haven't figured out why anyone would want to go flower shopping after dark, but hey, if she's interested, I'm willing to give it a shot."

Emma hadn't a clue who Rowena was but she *had* heard of the florist. "Nightshades? They grow the most amazing flowers there—the blooms are gorgeous and last practically forever."

Sam's brows rose. "The flowers are undying?"

"I believe the word you were looking for is 'undead,' and that, too, fits right in with Rowena's image," Lindsay added. "Although your choice of word does speak highly of you as a man, Huntingdon. When you mentioned undying, were you by any chance thinking of devotion?"

His gaze flicked toward Emma and she could swear she had actually *felt* it but she only returned his look with an empty stare.

"No, but now that you've brought it up, I think I will take Jordan with me when I go talk to Rowena. He can pick up something for Kaylee while we're there—as a token of *his* undying devotion to her, of course."

Lindsay and Sam's easy back and forth banter continued for a few minutes while Lindsay nursed her coffee. Finally, she pushed the cup aside and got to her feet. "Time to head out to my next appointment."

Sam stepped around her to collect her coat and held it out for her. "I'll call after I've seen Rowena. In the meantime, go ahead and put together a few sketches. I'm sure I can find someone who would be interested in renting out the second floor, even if it's just for office space."

"I really don't know why you didn't think of it before," Lindsay chided. "All that profitable floor space lying empty when you could have been collecting revenue from it every year since you first set up shop."

Emma saw him reach for her coat, presumably to help

her into it as he had done with Lindsay, and she snatched it out of his reach. Hurriedly shoving her arms inside, she preceded Lindsay to the door.

"It was a pleasure to make your acquaintance, Emma. Do stop in again soon for coffee," he called after her but she didn't stop, merely lifted her chin in the barest hint of a nod before pushing the door open and marching through.

Sam chuckled.

"Stiff little bit of a thing," he mused to Lindsay, who he noticed was also watching Emma walk away with a glimmer of curiosity in her eyes.

She grinned. "Yet another interesting choice of word and I'm just crazy enough to take a chance with mine and Emma's friendship to tell you why."

Sam held up a hand, stopping her. "Too much information. *Too much* information. I am sure whatever you are about to say will contain far too many details about at least one thing I definitely don't want to know."

Glancing to make sure Emma was far enough out of earshot to not hear what she was about to reveal, her delicately arched brow rose as Lindsay made her parting shot. "I'm willing to bet you would be a little *stiff* too, Sam Huntingdon, if you knew the kind of dreams Emma's been having since the two of you ran into each other at Seville's."

～

A SINGLE, perfect, blood-red bloom stood out against a web of greenery whose stems had been artfully tied with a matching red ribbon around a miniature bow hand-carved from the wood of a Hawthorne tree; it was the only warning the Seville sisters would receive.

Serephina knew it.

Mortianna knew it.

Esmerelda didn't understand how they knew, but the way her sisters were behaving after the departure of Rowena Bellaire, the owner of Nightshades—Hawthorne Grove's only after-hours florist, hand-delivered the blossom she was convinced it was true: the Cupid Heart Guard was coming—possibly for her—and it was all her fault.

Essentially, when she'd sold that darn quilt to the wrong woman, Esmerelda had broken some important codicil of the long-standing Cupid Pact—a mysterious contract of sorts which existed between her sisters and her and ... and she didn't even know who the other parties were!

Apparently, neither did her sisters.

"Why can't either of you tell me? Who are the members of this mysterious CHG organization and why must we cower or sit in judgment beneath them? What do they *do*? Are they some kind of ancient, all-mighty, supernatural witchy police force? Am I to be taken into custody?"

"Taken?" Serephina paled, hastily dropping down

onto the sofa while Mortianna clucked and soothed, trying to calm her.

"I'm sure it won't come to that, Merry," she soothed over her shoulder. "It *was* just a quilt, after all."

"Just a quilt?" Serephina's head came up. "That quilt was imbued with all the sensual emotion I could summon, and after years of rigidly enforced celibacy, I can assure you it was no small endowment! Not that it matters. Rather, Esmerelda, our problem comes from introducing our magic into the life of a woman for whom it was not intended."

Esmerelda shrugged. "So we made a mistake. Someone else falls in love after a few sensual dreams. Where is the harm in that?"

"It's not the *dreams*, dear," Mortianna explained, still using her soothing, unusually patient, mother hen tone of voice—mostly for Serephina's benefit, Esmerelda was sure. "It's the *emotion* behind those dreams. It needs to be channeled. To be directed. *Properly* directed—to its intended recipient."

"We *know* who purchased the darn thing. What is to stop us from giving a nudge here and there to make sure whatever *emotion* her dreams conjure is headed in the right direction?"

"That's just not the way it works. Not the way it works at all," Serephina moaned. "Why do you think I'm constantly nagging Morty to keep her fingers out of things once the magic has been cast? There are *conse-*

quences to meddling—consequences neither of us are prepared to handle."

"*What* consequences?" Esmerelda demanded, and when no answer was immediately forthcoming, she accused, "I don't believe you know. I don't believe either of you even remember. A pact, you say, that we all signed years ago—but you do not remember with whom the pact was made or even why? I'm calling hokey."

"Hokey?" Mortianna made a face at her juvenile name-calling of the sacred treatise she and her sisters had pledged their lives to. "Nothing about the Cupid Pact is hokey, Merry. It's … It's …"

"Yes? It's *what*?" When neither of her sisters rushed to inform her, Esmerelda adopted her best "I-did-what-neither-of-you-had-the-courage-to-do" stance and admitted, "I went to the archivists. Since neither of us can seem to recall the contents of precisely what we've signed or why, I decided it was time to find out. *That* is where I went while the two of you were in New York. I paid the Keeper a visit."

Mortianna's eyes went wide. "No! Esmerelda, you—you saw a Keeper of the Lore?"

Irritated now, Esmerelda narrowed her eyes and glared petulantly at her sister. "Yes, and so what? He isn't some untouchable, sacred deity, you know. Neither of them are."

"*Neither* of them? You mean you saw them both? No, that's not possible. So which did you see? Airrik or Alastair?"

"Does it matter?" Esmerelda snapped, quickly coming to the end of her rope with all this forbidden acts and horrible consequences chatter. "No, it doesn't. What matters here is that *finally* I will know what all the hoopla is about. I've requested a copy of the Pact. When I receive it, I intend to lock myself in my room until I've read every word—even the small print! I cannot stand this anymore. I have to know why it is so important for us to serve the whim and whimsy of this unknown Cupid Heart Guard."

"Why go to the Keepers, Merry?" Serephina asked, her voice both soft and weary. "Why didn't you simply ask *us*?"

"I *have!* All I get from the two of you is *Do as you're told, Merry. Don't upset the balance, Merry,*" she said, screwing up her face to add impact to her mimicry. "Well, now the balance is tipped and from what you two have told me there will be some dire and terrible conse-quence—only we don't know *what* or *why* or even *when*! But very well. If either of you know, tell me. Please. Tell me the terms of the Cupid Pact."

"Hold on. Hold on!" Mortianna demanded, pointed toward the scrying dish they'd hastily pulled back out after Ms. Bellaire's delivery from Nightshades. They were hoping for a heads up regarding the imminent arrival of the CHG but Mortianna could scarcely contain her excitement when she noticed Emma Riley heading into Sam's instead.

"Look! She's gone to the coffee shop. Guess last night

delivered one more dream than she could handle, huh, Serephina?"

"What do you mean?" Rising from the sofa, she pushed her sisters aside to peer into the dish and immediately turned away to wail. "Oh, no! I'm afraid we've made not just one mistake, sisters, but two."

Turning back to the scrying dish, she pointed one slim finger at the other woman in the scene. "Look there, at her wrist. How did we lose the charm bracelet, too?"

Esmerelda cast a quick glance but she wasn't worried about the bracelet. "Well at least we got our 214 to the right person this time—and we didn't even have to try!"

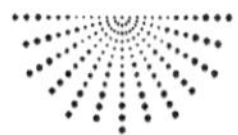

CHAPTER FIVE

"We close in five," Sam called out from behind the bar when he heard the front door open. He'd sent Gem home early and was just finishing putting away the last of today's mugs, cups, and assorted drinkware. "If you need it strong and black, we've got it, but other than that—"

Catching a glimpse from the corner of his eye of Emma standing uncertainly in the doorway caught him completely unaware and stole the words he'd been about to say. Surprise tinged his belated greeting. "Emma. Wow. Excuse me for saying so, but you're the last person I expected to see standing there when I turned around."

It was the truth. He'd figured Jordan had stopped in to give him a last minute update on his progress with the *chiffonier* before he picked up Kaylee headed into town for dinner and a movie. Seeing Emma instead had made him do a sort of double-take but she was definitely a welcome sight. A knit burgundy beret covered her hair and mauve colored gloves warmed her hands, one of which held her purse while the other clutched at a brown leather satchel and Sam's curiosity already on high alert, he wondered what secrets it hid about the lady who carried it at her side.

She had yet to move away from the door. In fact, she was standing with her hand still flattened on the frame like she wasn't sure whether or not she actually wanted to be there and was actually on the verge of leaving. Then, in what must have been a hard-won moment of decision for her, she took a few steps closer to the bar. "I—I couldn't sleep. I thought coffee might help."

She couldn't sleep? Confused, Sam cocked his head to the side and blinked a time or two. "Come again? Usually people come in here to wake up, not fall asleep."

"That was a joke." Emma lifted an eyebrow then she turned away, her chin dipping downward as her cheeks flushed to a still delicate but slightly brighter shade of peach and pink. Sam thought she might even have winced.

"Apparently a very bad one," she continued. "Sorry."

"No! No, don't apologize. I'm glad people feel comfortable enough with me to crack a joke now and then," he said, hoping a quick spate of chatter from him would give her time to recover from the temporary unease and embarrassment she obviously felt. Her chin rose a bit at that, and he smiled. "Lord knows I do enough of it myself. I just—I guess I wasn't really expecting humor from you. Threw me off my game."

Immediately, her eyes narrowed in speculation and he mentally closed his. Smacked his forehead a time or two, as well, but only in his imagination. *Oh, I'm an idiot.* Having pretty much declared he didn't find her humorous—at least as far as she seemed to be concerned—he realized he'd probably just dug for himself the beginnings of a huge, gaping hole he had a feeling would end up being very difficult to get out of once he fell in. "I—ah, I didn't actually mean that the way it came out."

"Of course not." Sam noticed she'd gone rigid. Her backbone was so stiff, if she sneezed it might snap, and her chin had gone up so high he wondered absently if she could even see him now.

"You would never actually *say* you find me less than amusing. Or anyone else for that matter," she added, and figuring it would be best to just keep his mouth shut for now, Sam waited, watching in silence as her expression slowly changed from one of offended hauteur to something a bit more polite and a tad bit apologetic and he wondered if she, too, had just realized she'd more or less admitted to thinking he didn't think much of her.

It wasn't true. Not at all. And knowing it wasn't might have been why he forgot about waiting, forgot to give her time to think about what they'd said and reassess his part of the conversation. It only took him a second, though, to realize he'd started running his mouth again in an attempt to smooth things over. "Hey, that really wasn't what I meant at all."

Tilting her head to one side, she peered up at him, her eyelids still narrowly slitted to allow for her pinning—or, more like *skewering*—glare. But something in the way her posture had changed made him think she wasn't as mad at him—or whatever she had been—now as she was a second ago.

"What *did* you mean?" she finally asked, and though this was something else about her he also hadn't expected, Sam realized she was serious. It seemed she was willing to admit she may have been wrong about her quick judgment of what he'd said and was giving him a chance to explain.

He felt his brows rise slightly in appreciation. He liked that kind of willingness in a woman.

Smiling again, partly because he found it easier to do than scowl and partly because doing it just came naturally to him, Sam hurried to explain himself—mostly so she would know *why* he'd said what he'd said—but also because he'd just this minute realized he wanted her to stay.

Explaining how he didn't do what she'd thought he had would certainly keep her in his store. For a few minutes anyway. *If* he could stretch his explanation out that long—and he was definitely going to try.

"You aren't Lindsay," he blurted out, then he stopped in mid-conversation, half-turned away from her and rolled his eyes at his own gaff and muttered, "*What am I, stupid? Of course she's not Lindsay!*" before he faced her again with what he hoped was a slightly embarrassed but completely earnest expression. "What I mean to say is, you're *you*. Emma. The Research Analyst, right?"

"Freelance Research Specialist," she corrected. "And you're not doing yourself any favors here. Why is it perfectly alright for Lindsay to have a sense of humor but not I—or ... er, me—or whatever the correct way to say that is."

Sam laughed. "See? Now *that* is the type humor I *would* have expected from you. You're a word girl, right?"

When she nodded—albeit slowly—Sam hastened to continue. "Lindsay, she's not."

Taking the chance that Emma was interested enough in his explanation not to balk when he reached for her hand, Sam caught her fingers and led her to a table in the semi-circular morning nook where the curtains were still open and she could look out into the night while he would be rewarded with perfect views of her every feature reflected all around the room.

"Don't get me wrong. I love Lindsay to pieces, but she's a bit of a—she's like a *diva*, I guess you'd call her, mostly for lack of a better word," he admitted somewhat boyishly. "And because I didn't want to say she's a drama queen. That is definitely what she's *not*," he finished, emphasizing the point with a shake of his finger before cocking his head thoughtfully to one side.

"Lindsay—*hmm*. She's more of a flirt and flutter girl, you know what I mean? While *you* ..." Her hand was still resting loosely in his and Sam lifted it, waiting, watching her until their gazes caught. Slowly, carefully so as not to frighten her away before he could finish his explanation, he swirled the pad of his thumb in a light circle across her palm and said, "I think you're more a dream and sigh kind of lady and more than a little bit shy."

Emma immediately attempted to retrieve her hand from his but Sam caught it again before she could stand and take flight. With his eyes, he willed her to stay and to tell him the truth while his lips asked, "Am I right?"

How could he read her so easily? She had never been what people would call an open book although she had never been all that expressive, either. But what had he called her? A dream and sigh kind of lady? That actually seemed to fit. It flustered her, the depth of his insight, so much she almost forgot why she stopped by.

"Queens didn't drink coffee," she blurted instead of answering his far too probing question, and reached for the bag at her side. Digging inside the leather case, she pulled out the document she had prepared and handed it over to him. "At least not from your service, I think."

Unable to keep from glancing up at him to see his reaction, she furtively met his eyes. There were questions in his gaze which she ignored as much as the uncomfortable sense of embarrassment she felt beginning to rise. "While you and Lindsay were discussing the renovations, I sort of became fascinated with the coffee set." She explained with a shrug. Handing over the papers, she looked away to avoid whatever censure she might see in his eyes."I did a little research. The service you have is genuine Meissen and should probably be in a museum but—this is the bulk of my find."

Uncomfortable waiting in the drawn out silence while he flipped through the pages, Emma stood and walked to the wide bank of windows looking out over the shop's south side.

In her mind she could picture cozy little structures tucked into spaces between the tall trees, mini-gazebos or something with steep Victorian roofs beneath which one could sit with a friend or two and chat while their coffee cooled or sit alone and avail themselves of the already on offer free WiFi. She imagined padded benches inside, with snuggly wraps and brilliantly colored big fluffy throw pillows waiting on every side.

Emma could easily see herself happily ensconced in such a nook, reading a book while she sipped at her coffee. Too bad her sketch pad was in her briefcase which was too close to Sam right now. Glancing over her shoulder to find him still examining the papers and sketches she'd brought, she said, "The view from the windows is beautiful, Mr. Huntingdon. Have you considered putting tables out there?"

There was a half-distracted look about him when he lifted his gaze. "What did you have in mind?"

Emma considered whether it would be easier for her to tell him her thoughts, or simply show him instead. If she opened her mouth she knew she would end up tongue-tied but sketching would require sitting close to him again and she didn't know if she could do so without becoming lost in the sensual world of her dreams and with him so near she was almost terrified she might invite him to join her inside.

"Emma?" He prompted, looking over the papers at her. "You had an idea? I'd love to know what you had in mind."

His gentle urging was all she needed. Retracing her steps to the table, she sat down and reached for her bag again. "I'll show you."

Taking out a sketch pad and pencil, she began to draw what she had seen in her thoughts whenever she'd looked out over the frost-covered grounds outside. Before she knew it Emma became lost in her task, her fingers flying across the page and back again until she forgot where she was and exactly who sat watching and looking with curious awe at her from the table's other side. Finally, though, her fingers slowed and reality encroached upon the scene in which she had been living in her mind.

Lifting her head, she saw the most intriguing look on Sam's face. She flushed, first hot and then cold, and her fingers started to shake so she hastily laid her pencil aside. Embarrassed to have intruded yet again where she did not belong, Emma sought to cover her reaction by reaching down for the satchel at her feet.

"I'm sorry, Mr. Huntingdon. Truly, I am. I don't know why I thought you would be interested in this, or *these*," she said, indicating both her research and the sketch she had just made with a dismissing wave of her hand. "I—I just see things in my head sometimes."

But when she reached out for the sketch book to put it away, his hand came down, covering hers and something crazy happened to her inside. The room grew hot and her breathing slowed while her heartbeat seemed to triple. Frozen, stunned, and a little terrified, Emma slowly lifted her head until her gaze met his and she gasped at the wonder and curiosity, the intense interest and awe she saw radiating from his eyes.

"You are an intelligent and amazingly talented woman, Miss Riley. Why in the world do you try so hard to hide it?" he said, touching her with the sincerity of his words and tone and then Emma was falling into the dream before she could blink or do anything to break its untimely spell.

Had he felt the way she was trembling? Was that why he took her hand? Did she moan out loud or was it a gasp from her lips that had brought him to his feet, she wondered from deep in the haze that was once her thoughts but where now her desires held sway—the real world of ever-suppressed need and yearning and hope called reality had come abruptly to an end.

Emma really didn't know how it happened but she was suddenly on her feet, standing clutched to his body within the circle of his arms and her fingers were threaded through his hair. And then sometime, somewhere between one breath and the next his lips touched hers and she knew. Emma knew that she was lost—*so lost*.

Her normal self was suddenly up and gone and the woman left in her place wasn't scared.

The normal Emma—the timid, aloof, mousy little Emma most of the world knew had disappeared. She was sucked unexpectedly into the primal vortex of her soul to that place where dream became reality and reality a dream—and it was there where Emma completely lost her head.

Ignoring the tiny voice of warning that told her she was about to do something she'd regret, Emma gave herself over to his kiss. Relaxing into his embrace, she kissed him back, reveling in the moment—one she knew she would never forget. Sam's lips were warm, his body warmer, and his touch where his fingers caressed the sensitive area of skin at the base of her skull was slowly lulling her into …

Thump, thump, thump.

The muted but unmistakable sound of someone thumping a fist somewhere nearby intruded on Emma's thoughts but she didn't want the kiss to end. Squeezing her eyelids tightly closed, she wished the momentarily unwanted intrusion away but the thump became a pounding instead.

"Sam? Hey Sammy, you in there, man? I can see the lights, so I know you are there somewhere. Come unlock the door and hurry up! Kaylee's about to freeze out here!"

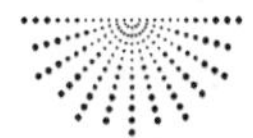

CHAPTER SIX

Sam slowly opened his eyes, finally realizing the pounding noises he was hearing in the back of his mind wasn't the blood rushing to his head. Still, he fought to ignore the incessant, pounding bid for his attention, preferring to explore the exciting revelation in Emma's passion-filled kisses instead. But it was not to be. Eyes open now, his gaze locked with Emma's and he knew *she* knew they'd been caught. Her eyes had gone wide and were suddenly clear; no longer dazed by passion.

"The front door, it's still *open*," she whispered urgently against his now still lips and Sam froze, his own gaze flying to the door in question. Finding she was right, he groaned in frustrated disappointment and disentangling her fingers from where she'd buried them in his hair, he pulled away with an apologetic half-smile.

"If I asked you to wait while I got rid of them, would

you?" he tried, but was pretty sure he already knew what her answer would be—if he moved away from Emma right now he knew she would take up her things and flee, disappearing long before he could make it back to her side because the blush on her cheeks was already an unusually fiery red and she refused to meet his gaze.

Pulling away, she scrambled to gather her purse and satchel; the sketch papers she left where they lay. "I can't, Sam. I'm—I'm really sorry but I have to go. This—I—this was a mistake," she whispered the last, then covered her face with her hands and added, mostly to herself, "*Oh Lord, such a massively* huge *mistake! Please, please. If there's a God in Heaven, just please. let. me. die.*"

"Emma, wait—" Sam started, taking two steps toward her, but she stopped him with a frantic shake of her head and then turned and practically ran out the front door of the shop to her car outside. His gut told him he probably should have followed her then but another round of thumping from the access door off the kitchen had him turning in the other direction.

As soon as he unlocked the deadbolt, Kaylee and Jordan rushed in. "Sammy, what in the world were you doing in there? Don't tell me we caught you on the john," Jordan teased with a grin but Sam was still too caught up in what had just happened to think of a suitably snappy comeback.

In the middle of slipping out of her apple green pea coat, Kaylee turned and gave her *fiance* a truly horrified look before she swatted at his arm and sighed. "Jordan! I swear, that's just gross," she said before turning a narrow-eyed glare on Sam. "Don't you dare try to answer him, either, because I don't want to know. You two still act like children sometimes."

"Which is part of my manly appeal, admit it," Sam heard Jordan saying behind him but he'd already moved off, heading back to the main area, hoping to use their momentary distraction of removing coats and gloves to scoop up the sketches and documents Emma had left behind. The faint scent of her perfume still lingered in the air when he bent over the table to collect the pages. Desire hit him hard, slammed him right in the gut, and all he could do was grunt and sigh. Gathering the pages, he quickly leaned half over the bar and slid everything on a shelf behind it.

"What took you so long, anyway?" Jordan asked curiously as him and Kaylee joined Sam in the main room now, their outerwear removed.

Resting casually against the bar now that he'd cleared away the evidence of his previous company, Sam lifted a hand and pointed with one finger to the spot where he and Emma had been standing only a moment or two before.

"I was making out with a beautiful woman, actually, right there in the middle of the room," he quipped, making sure to inject a hint of playfulness into his tone as he did so because he knew exactly what they would hear if he did. The slightly silly-ish edge of humor in his tone would do its part to convince them he was joking.

Letting his brows lower into a ferocious mock scowl, he grouched, "Then you two showed up and Jordan went and scared her away with all his thumping on the door and dad-blasted yelling."

Feeling more than a little pleased with himself that he was able to be fairly honest with his friends—it *was* mostly just a kiss he and Emma had shared, after all—Sam's conscience was fairly gleaming. Still, he had a gut feeling if Jordan and Kaylee hadn't interrupted, their kiss could have become so much more. An image of *doing more* with Emma flashed through his thoughts and a sudden, unexpected surge of straight up lust hit him hard —and his body's immediate physical reaction made him spin back around toward the bar to hide the visual evidence of his unusually out of control desire.

Picking up the rag he had forgotten there earlier, Sam vigorously scrubbed at the already spotless surface the bar. Once or twice as he did so, his gaze slid with longing toward the front door through which Emma had made her escape. Half wishing she would come back even though he knew she would not, he forced the crazy idea from his thoughts, drew in a somewhat steadying breath, and turned his gaze once more on Jordan and Kaylee.

"So what are you two doing here?" he asked in a reasonably normal tone, but then something bright and familiar dangling from Kaylee's hand caught his now undivided attention.

"Was the woman you were making out with wearing a beret and mauve colored gloves, Sam?" she asked, the items in question held up between one thumb and a finger while she peered at him in stunned surprise.

Sam's earlier good humor vanished; it simply drained away as he jolted into action. Stomping around the bar to her side, he practically snatched the garments from Kaylee while surreptitiously sliding another glance toward the front door. Then, just as uncharacteristically gruff, he rounded the bar again to put Emma's hat and gloves with the sketches and stuff he'd already slid out of sight, muttering, "That would be the one, yes."

Well, now he was cornered. They were caught, even if Emma was technically not there and no longer available for apprehending. Ignoring the curious speculation in both his friends eyes, he desperately tried to think what —or, more specifically, how much—about Emma's visit he should tell them. There was no way he could hide the fact that she had actually been there now, and while he figured Jordan might let him keep his secrets for a while, he knew Kaylee would never let it slide. Not when it came to him being with a woman.

Propping his hands solidly on the smooth surface of the bar, he faced their obviously drawn conclusions head-on while doing his best to pretend not to care. Leaning slightly forward, he conceded an admission, "You two just missed her, actually. She just ran out the door and her name is Emma, Kaylee. Emma Riley. Do you either of you already know her?"

Jordan cast a speaking look at Kaylee then dropped his gaze to the floor while his lips worked to hold back a grin. Finally, his brows arched high, and he let out a slow little whistle before looking at Sam again. "Wow, Sammy. I don't know what to say. But her name is awfully close to Ellie."

~

AT HOME, Emma snatched the quilt from her bed and flung it as hard as she could into the farthest corner of her bedroom while muttering, "Stupid dreams! Stupid quilt! And stupid, *stupid* Emma!" Flopping dejectedly down onto the now unmade and disheveled side of her bed, she covered her face with both of her hands in abject humiliation.

"How *could* I have done it? *Why* did I do it? Why? Why? *Why*?" Slapping her hands down onto her thighs, she demanded of no one, "What heretofore unknown demon of insanity could possibly have possessed me to get up from that chair and kiss him like that?"

Meow.

Lowering her hands, Emma flung a sullen glance at the quilt in the corner and found Chloe quietly pawing and tugging at the probably priceless antique. She'd climbed squarely into the middle of it and was even now dancing in circles between the wrinkles and folds, trying to make a more comfy bed from it for herself.

Emma frowned. "Careful, Chloe, that thing is detritus. Rubbish," she continued, her tone filled with spite. "Foul and quite possibly sneaky. Trust me, girl. You take it from me. You shouldn't soil your dainty little claws on it."

There was far too much disdain in her tone, she realized. Especially for a quilt. But from the moment she'd first lain her hands on the thing she'd been tormented by visions and tortured by dreams—all of them co-starring Sam. *Why?*

"Why would a quilt make me think of him, Chloe? I mean, we'd never even met before."

"*Meow.*"

"And then suddenly he's kissing me in my dreams? Something has to be going on here."

"*Meow.*"

"Maybe I'm cursed and I just don't know it," Emma whispered, walking over to her dresser to study herself in the mirror. Her normal reflection stared back and she went back to the bed again only this time she lay across it so that she was closer to the quilt—no, *Chloe*—in the corner. "I certainly don't look like I'd be the type to throw myself at a man, so why in the world *did* I?"

"*Meow!*"

Lying there trying to find reasons for her unforgivable and utterly immoral behavior, Emma slowly became aware that the scent of Sam's cologne was all around her —it was emanating from her clothes. They smelled of decadence and exotic coffee and a bit of rich chocolate, too—all things which made her hungry for his kisses and more—of his touch, of his body, too. There was simply no denying it—what she wanted was more of *him.*

Frowning now, she rolled onto her side and stared off at nothing, but her head was still full of Sam. No wonder she'd completely lost her mind with him—he'd taken control of her senses!

"*Meow.*"

"Still won't be going back there, though," she muttered, and she meant it. Her embarrassment would simply kill her. Besides, there was simply no need. "I left the sketches behind for him. I'm sure he'll feel free to use them."

It felt good to know Sam Huntingdon had everything he needed if he wanted to do as she had suggested he should—and she really hoped he would do so. The Victorian-themed gazebo-like nooks would be lovely come springtime when the flowers began to bloom and her ideas were perfect for a bit of outdoor expansion. They were also in keeping with Lindsay's plans for his renovation and any architectural designer worth his or her salt could take what she'd drawn and create a set of prints for him.

Her mind already spinning with thoughts and scenes of what Sam might create with her drawings, Emma rolled over onto her back and closed her eyes while she ran her fingers through her hair, combing away the gnarls and tangles. Unconsciously, she spread the length of it over the edge of her mattress and the side of the bed, letting it spill onto the floor—and was immediately struck with a vision of Sam leaning over her there, joining her on the bed.

With a gasp of shock, she sprang up from the mattress and rounded the bed where she stopped and glared at Chloe. The cat had managed to work the quilt out of the corner and over to the side of the bed—it was lying right where her hair must have fallen, but...

Shooing Chloe off the thing, Emma bent and picked it up to fold it. Tomorrow, she would call Lindsay and ask her to come by and pick it up, then drop it off at the coffee shop for Sam. Glaring at Chloe, she said, "Naughty girl. You did that on purpose, didn't you? I know you like it and it is nice and soft, but I don't want it anymore."

"*Meeeoooww.*"

Arching a brow at the feline, she wondered how it was even possible for a cat to sound morose but Chloe certainly had. Tossing the quilt onto her dresser, Emma shook her head at Chloe and shut off her bedroom light then went into the living room to sulk. Or pine. Or whatever a woman as confused and still wound up inside from the sensual feast and pleasurable delight she'd found in Sam's kisses usually did.

From the corner of her eye, she caught a glimpse of the edge of the puzzle box she'd picked up at Seville's—it was still lying on the table by her white glazed French doors where she'd put it the day she bought it and then promptly forgot it was there. *Because of the dreams*, her treacherous mind taunted.

Shaking her head she felt her cheeks heat with remembered pleasure brought on by the memory of his kiss. But memories of what she had done tonight with

Sam—without any prior sort of provocation from him—brought back the agonizing guilt and utter mortification she'd felt, too, and she really didn't want to deal with those right now.

Pushing the irritating reminders away, she walked over and took up the box. A puzzle could be exactly what she needed right now. The level of concentration required to put it together should certainly prove a more than welcome distraction from her now ever constant thoughts of Sam. At least she'd thought it would, but when she opened the box, the first thing she saw was a card lying atop the intricately carved puzzle pieces just beneath the lid.

Curious, she picked it up to examine, then immediately let out a groan of frustration. Etched into the surface in bold, black lettering were the words: *Huntingdon's One Stop Coffee Shop*. And there was a picture of a steaming mug of coffee. It was *his* card and she knew someone had put it in the puzzle box on purpose but what she couldn't figure out was *who* or *when*.

Deep in thought, trying to figure it out, Emma ran a finger over the raised lettering for a moment then flipped the card around. On the back was a number, written in ink, and probably by his own hand. Was this his actual personal number? She wondered. There were a couple of things about him she probably really should know—like whether or not he was married. Lindsay had never mentioned it to her, but then, she never mentioned lots of things.

Staring at the numbers, Emma couldn't stop herself from wondering—if she called the number on the back of the card would he be the one to answer? Or would it be picked up by his wife instead? Ignoring the quick rush of immediate horror she felt at the thought she might have kissed a married man, Emma hastily laid the card aside and picked up the puzzle box instead. The last thing she needed to see or do right now was anything related to Sam. Hadn't she gotten herself into enough trouble over him already?

CHAPTER SEVEN

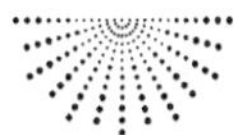

*C*arefully sealing the iron-banded door behind him with the whispered archaic words of a ward as he stepped through and into the Hawthorne Grove Public Library, Alastair Skurlocke cast a sidelong glance at the tall walnut and brass clock in the corner. He hoped he hadn't kept Esmerelda waiting.

With any luck, he thought, hurrying out the front door to the lighted walk beyond, she would not yet be here. He needed time with her—time alone—to tell her what he had learned. She was not going to like what he had to say, or even what he then must do once she appeared, but he had been commanded by one of great power. *Bring her to me,* the whispers had said, and he would not disobey.

Alastair had barely cleared the front walk when the click of heels on the stones before him signaled Esmerelda's arrival. Drawing up, he paused beneath a light to await her while questioning himself once more. Before he handed her over, he must be sure he was doing the right thing.

"Did you get it?" she asked the instant she saw him; her eyes were brimming with both hope and expectation —both of which he knew he would soon crush, for he truly had nothing to give her. The difficult part, however, was going to be the explanation for why.

Hesitant now, he tried to stave off the dreaded revelation of what he had found for as long as he possibly could. "You must be aware that magical lore is enchanted. Such documents would need to be translated before you could possibly read it."

Her frown said she was not happy to learn this but she would not let the delay sway her decision to find out what was in the long-ago archived mystical document she had requested he find. "Who do I need to see for that?"

Alastair sighed. He should have known she would not be deterred. Esmerelda Seville was nothing if not pertinacious once she set her mind to a course of action. Nothing he said to her would matter at this point. She was clearly determined to see this through. Resigned that there was no other way, he opted for the truth. "No one as it turns out. Esmerelda, I regret to be the one to inform you of this, but there is no such thing as a Cupid Pact."

Like the response from having flipped a switch, her

spine stiffened and her lids narrowed over her eyes. "There *is*."

"No, there truly is not. Nor is there, to our especial knowledge, any magic council or committee, or assemblage of supernatural administrators known as the CHG —" he started in an attempt to explain but she was no longer listening.

Stalking past him she made for the library—likely she meant to try and seek out Airrick inside.

"You can't. The guards will stop you unless I am there by your side. You know this," he reminded softly as he fell into step beside her. "Esmerelda, stop. Will you wait a minute, please? Look, I'm sorry I don't have what you're looking for but I would still like to help you."

She drew up so suddenly he almost walked past her. "Help me what? If there is no Cupid Pact, no CHG, there was nothing to come here for. Right?" There were tears in her eyes and he could easily imagine why. To think so many years of her life might have been wasted ... if someone had told him the same of himself, it might well have made him want to cry.

But the moment wasn't over yet. There was still more he had yet to do. He had to tell her something, though, before he escorted her inside. She deserved at least that much warning, though he knew she would not like it. "Esmerelda, I think you and your sisters are in trouble."

"That's enough, Skurlocke. We have no time," came a voice to his ear on the wind. *"You must bring her to me—now.*

Alastair obediently nodded—or was it a bow he made into the night?—then reached down to take Esmerelda's hand, carefully linking her fingers through his. For whatever reason, Esmerelda Seville had been summoned and he would see her brought safely to the man he knew awaited her presence inside. Motioning with one hand for silence, he signaled for Esmerelda to follow him back into the library and then through the secret door, after which he led her immediately into a dark and sparsely furnished chamber off the long central corridor.

"Wait here. You're safe, Esmerelda. I promise," he said, and quickly closed the door behind him, leaving her alone in the darkness.

∾

ESMERELDA HAD BEEN certain Alastair was about to take her into the chambers below and deliver the Cupid Pact —the document she had come here for. But when she heard him whispering outside the door, she knew she would not be able to leave the chamber unless or until he allowed it.

The chamber had been warded—and by Keeper magic at that.

Spinning about in the now darkened room, she pounded her fists against the door. "Blast you, Alastair Skurlocke! Let me out of here now!"

When that did not seem to work, she tried another angle. "Mortianna and Serephina both know where I am.

They *will* come looking for me!"

It was true. Her sisters did know she had come to the Keeper and they would eventually pay him a visit, too—if he didn't let her out soon. But then, she remembered she need not have worried. He would not keep her here forever. The Keeper's chambers were sacrosanct and she had invaded that space. Was, in fact, breaking rules right and left just by being here.

After taking a moment to calm down and regroup, she realized he was simply trying to protect her. "Still, the room leaves something to be desired," she muttered as she looked around the small space. There were no windows in the chamber and yet it was not quite utterly dark. From somewhere, a glimmer of light in the shadows allowed her to see an old workbench upon which sat an unlit candle. There was also one slightly askew but still perfectly serviceable chair.

Glaring back over her shoulder at the warded door, Esmerelda decided to use a little magic of her own. She waved her fingers and whispered a few words, then stood back and admired the scene she had created with delight. Gone were the shadows and the smell of non-use. From one instant to the next, the darkness was gone and in its place the cheery light of a crackling fire—one she'd spelled into the wall across from the chair. It *was* cool out tonight, after all.

The workbench had transformed into a rich wooden desk and the lone candle, too, was gone. In it's place sat a gleaming three-armed brass candelabra. Another whisper, another snap, and she had everything she needed—for as long as he made her wait.

A bowl of fruit, a half-read book, and green and gold plaid chenille throw for her lap would be plenty to keep her cozy. At least for a little while. If Alastair did not come back for her soon, she would have to find her way out. For now, however, she was content to read while he did what he had to to make her presence here okay with the guards.

As she settled into the chair and picked up her book, she wondered what he was doing and how long it would take. If she didn't return pretty soon, Mortianna and Serephina really would start to worry. Glancing at the magically placed ornate clock on the mantel she mentally checked the time. One hour, she decided. She would give Alastair one hour to do what he needed, then—her thoughts broke off suddenly as the room became awash in a sudden shower of brilliant white light.

Lifting a hand to shield her eyes, she leaned to the side to try and get a better view of whatever magical being had found their way into this warded room. Slowly, the light began to dim, to reveal the shape of a man. He was tall, she noticed right away, though very oddly dressed. As her eyes adjusted she saw he had long, golden hair which brought to mind the majestically flowing mane of a lion—it spilled across the breadth of his very broad shoulders.

"Hello Esmerelda," he said and she caught herself rising for he was definitely one she dared not offend. His voice was like that of an hundred angels, his gaze direct though surprisingly warm. His stance was commanding, the same as his presence, and she assumed he must be the one she had been so desperately reluctant but destined to face.

"Do I know you?" she asked, still hoping to delay the inevitable.

Though his reaction barely registered upon his visage, she thought she saw a hint of surprise. "Know me? How could you not?"

So it was him, she realized dejectedly. The leader of the CHG. Now she knew why Alastair had locked her in, but it hadn't helped. Her moment of truth had come. Straightening her shoulders, Esmerelda lifted her chin and faced him with more bravado than might. "I'm sorry I messed up with the quilt. I'm sorry if I broke the Pact. But surely you see we have served faithfully and well. It *has* been twenty seven years after all. Can you not simply let us be?"

Golden brows drew downward and his eyelids narrowed over his beautiful sapphire eyes. "What quilt? What pact?"

With a frown of her own, Esmerelda backed away. "You're not him? You did not—come here for me? Wait. Who are you? I do not understand."

"It's a spell," the man uttered, and then stepped forward to place his fingers upon her forehead. "*Et umbrae,*" he quietly whispered the Latin and stunned,

Esmerelda realized she knew the meaning, without any explanation at all.

Let the shadows fall, he'd said, and so they certainly had! "Oh *no*. Oh no! I have to get back. I must warn Morty and Serephina!"

Only she never made it to tell them—never took one step from the room because in one instant her heels were clicking on the stones of the floor and in the next, she was suddenly gone.

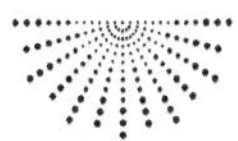

CHAPTER EIGHT

*L*indsay looked over the antique woodcut puzzle and frowned. "Let me see if I have this right. You know there is a piece missing but you aren't going to go back to Seville's and complain because you know where the piece is. You just refuse to go get it."

Emma's expression was a bit mulish. "Yes, that's about it."

For a minute, Lindsay simply stared at her in silence, blinking now and then, until she finally sighed and straightened out of the hunched over position she'd been standing in to point out how silly her friend was being. "Emma, you can't leave a puzzle unfinished! Especially if you don't have to. It's—It's just wrong!"

"I can and I am," Emma told her. Unfolding her legs from beneath her, she got up off the couch and came up beside Lindsay to collect the pieces of the almost completed puzzle. Dumping them into the box, she asked over her shoulder, "Why did you say you stopped by again? I know it wasn't to harangue me over my puzzle but I can't remember now after all that grumping you did over one little missing piece."

Lindsay wanted to smack her—or to smack her own forehead, or something. Why did Emma always pretend issues were little? Granted, it was just a puzzle they were talking about now but she did it with all sorts of important things. Like her unnecessary avoidance of Sam Huntingdon, for one. "You need to call Sam. Or go by the One Shot. He really, really wants to talk to you about something only he won't tell me what. He just says it's confidential." Peering at her friend, she asked, "Did you and Sam do something confidential when I wasn't looking?"

Emma scoffed. "Of course not." Her puzzle collected, Emma slid the top onto the box and headed to the kitchen. "You want coffee?"

"No, no time for it," Lindsay declined. "I'm supposed to be on my way out of town right now but Sam was adamant I stop by." Pinning Emma with a look, she said, "I know there's something going on between you two that you're not telling me. I will find out, Emma Riley. Just like I found out about..."

Emma handed her a steaming cup and carried her own back to the sofa where she sat once again with her legs crossed beneath her yoga style. "I did some research, okay? The day you and I were in the shop and he showed us the coffee service, I was intrigued."

Lindsay considered for a moment, then shook her head. "Nope. No, that's not it. Sam's not the type to get all antsy over a little porcelain history. What aren't you telling me?"

Emma made a face. "Anything that's none of your business."

Lindsay sipped at her coffee. "Fine. Fine. You try and keep your secrets and I swear I won't tell you another thing about Trace."

Trace Walker was a single hottie who had just moved into Hawthorne Grove and had all the young ladies gawking. Particularly Lindsay, but mostly because she thought the guy would be perfect for Emma.

Resting her forehead on her fingertips, Emma rolled her eyes. "I think I shall survive."

"You can try." Lindsay went into the kitchen to put her cup on the counter. "I have to run now, sweetie, but you know he's going to call me and ask if I came by and I'm going to have to tell him something."

"Tell him you came by."

"He is going to want to know if I delivered his message."

"So tell him you did."

"Are you going to call him, then?"

"Not in this lifetime," Emma offered sweetly and Lindsay growled in annoyance.

"I swear, Emma, you're going to drive me insane."

"No, you're going to drive yourself that way if you keep trying to convince me to do things I have no intention of doing. I'm pretty sure you're going to be late, too. Didn't you tell me you have somewhere to be?"

Glancing at her watch, Lindsay gasped. "Yes! Yes, I do and as bad as I hate to drink and run, if I don't get out of here now I'm never going to make it!" Gathering up her purse, she dashed for the door, calling over her shoulder to Emma, "Call Sam! Whatever it is he wants to talk to you about must be pretty important."

To him, Emma thought sourly as the door closed behind Lindsay. Still, her gaze skittered to her purse and she thought of the card inside. Maybe she should call him, if for nothing more than to demand he return her puzzle piece. But even the thought of speaking to him after what she had done was so mortifying she could not summon the courage to call. The mere idea of getting into her car to drive by made her break out in a nervous sweat.

"Why are you doing this to me?" she demanded of no one because there was no one around to demand. No one other than Chloe, who was currently busy eyeing her with disdain while she waited to see whether or not Emma would give in to her fears or her fantasies. Emma's sullen glare should have been answer enough for the cat, but still she said, "Fear wins."

She didn't know why she was still so embarrassed over the kissing incident, though. Days had passed and the world had not exploded nor had it opened up a great, gaping hole with which to swallow her through. As for Sam Huntingdon, he had probably already forgotten what had happened … but if he had, why was he so adamant Lindsay talk her into calling him?

"Probably wants to bother me about that quilt," she decided.

He knew she had it just like she knew he had her puzzle piece. Maybe he wanted to do a trade?

Just thinking about the quilt and the dreams she'd had about Sam while sleeping under it made her cheeks go warm but despite her decision to the contrary, she still had the thing. Emma was fully aware she could have given the quilt to Lindsay days ago and asked her to give it to Sam but for some reason she did not want to explore right now, she was actually reluctant to get rid of it.

"*Meow,*" she heard right before Chloe streaked across the room and onto the table by the door—and then Emma froze, her mouth half-open in a muted gasp of annoyed horror as her purse lost most of its contents during its free fall to the floor. Springing up from the couch, she stared at the cat in stunned dismay.

"Chloe, *why*? Bad, bad kitty!" she admonished and hurried over to pick up the mess. On the top of the pile lay the card she had been avoiding. Looking over her shoulder, she glared at the cat and accused, "You're as bad as Lindsay!"

Rocking back on her heels, she groaned. "I don't want to call him! I don't want to hear the rich timber of his voice or imagine the look in his eyes when I say hello or to think about how nice it felt to sink my fingers into his hair while his sifted tenderly through mine." That was the way she imagined it, at least. He might have had any number of descriptions for what he'd been doing with his fingers in her hair in mind.

"None of which I want to know!" she blurted to Chloe but she knew as well as the now primly posturing feline was a lie. Beyond annoyed with the whole situation, she stuffed her belongings back inside her purse—including the card—and then she pulled it back out again. "Fine. I will call him. And then both you and Lindsay can bug me all you want to because I won't be doing anything like this again!"

Maybe it wasn't such a bad idea to call, Emma thought, just because. If a woman answered, well, at least she would know. She stretched an arm toward the table to grab her cell phone and then quickly dialed the number that was scrawled across the back of the card.

"One Stop. This is Sam. What can I do for you today?"

Just the sound of his voice made her pulse throb, exactly the way she had feared it would do. Emma closed her eyes.

"Hello? Hello? Is anyone there?" There was a long moment of silence, and then, "Press one if you can hear me."

Instantly, Emma recognized the line from one of those macho-type movies her brothers liked. She couldn't quite hold back her snort of laughter—or was it actually more a giggle? "Gone in Sixty Seconds," she blurted the way she did with her brothers—guessing which lines came from what movies was a familiar game they played—but she instantly regretted the impulse.

"Emma? Emma is this actually you? Finally! I've been trying to get in touch with you for a week now!"

Ignoring the smirkish twist her lips automatically curled into, she said, "Yes. It's me, but I'm surprised you remembered I had a name. It's the quilt you wanted me to call you about, right? Well, I'm letting you know you can have the thing. Lindsay will bring it by tomorrow."

Without another word she ended the call and then tossed her phone onto the sofa before drawing up her knees to make a pillow for her head. Why couldn't she just be like her brothers, who never worried about this sort of thing? William or even Tyler would have done what they wanted and hang what tomorrow might bring. But not Emma. No, not sweet, shy little worry wart Emma.

At that moment, she suddenly felt more alone and disconnected—from her family, from her friends, from anyone who might have loved her whom with the exception of Lindsay was absolutely no one—than she had in years.

Beside her, the ringer on her cell phone pealed, jerking her out of her moment of misery. With hands gone unsteady, she reached over and flipped it to look at the caller id—it was Sam. Pressing the button to decline the call, she got up and went to the kitchen. She would eat, and then she would read. Or start to work on the puzzle again. But she hadn't gone a handful of steps before her phone went off again.

It was him again and for a moment Emma thought about blocking his number. Instead, she slid her thumb across the screen, put the thing to her ear, and waited for him to speak.

"Emma, I need to talk to you—not about the quilt though we can discuss that, too, but about the things you left on my table."

"They're yours," she said. "I don't need them anymore." Her voice was barely above a whisper.

"Thank you. I appreciate your permission, but I really need a signature. Are you available right now? Wait. You don't have to come all the way out here. I will drive out and meet you—just tell me when and where."

"My signature? Why on earth would you need that? It was nothing but research and half a handful of drawings."

"Yes, all of which are valuable intellectual property, Emma, and yours specifically. Not mine, although I would love to—never mind that right now. May I have your address please?"

No! she wanted to yell. The last thing she needed right now was for Sam to pop up on her doorstep but she had to admit she was intrigued. "Look, Mr. Huntingdon, you have my permission to use the documents and drawings. I don't need to see you to give that."

"That may be true, but—dammit, Emma! We need to

talk about the papers, yes, but did you ever consider I might actually just want to see you?"

Pulling the phone away from her ear, she stared at it as if it were foreign and poison for a second before slowly replacing it to whisper, "No, the thought never crossed my mind."

But even as the words left her mouth, she knew she was outright lying—to herself and to him because for him to want to see her again was the one thing she secretly had wished for. But every time Lindsay mentioned him she said only that Sam wanted her to call. Was it possible he had used the research as an excuse to see her again?

Through the phone, she heard him sigh, and imagined he was rubbing muscles at his neck to relieve the sudden tension. "Well, I did and I do. I *need* to see you, actually, and not just for business reasons. I've barely thought of anything else since you left me the other night."

Since she'd left him? How did he manage to make it sound like she had done him some grievous injury? "It was late and I had to get home. Plus, your shop was closed, remember?"

He was silent for a moment and Emma thought he might give up—and she knew she didn't really want him to. Thinking quickly, she glanced over at her mail and gave him the first address she saw and then twisted her arm so she could see her watch. It was almost six thirty. "I'm at 1423 Brecker Street but I'll only be here until seven."

"Got it. Thanks," he said, his tone a bit distracted, and then he chuckled deep—it was an immensely pleasurable sound. "I'll be there in less than ten minutes."

He ended the call leaving Emma confused. What had he found so amusing? Frowning, Emma snatched up the envelope and immediately felt like an idiot—first class. *Oh, no. Did I really? I couldn't have*! But she had—she had given him the address for the shop where she occasionally ordered lingerie and now Sam was on his way there. To meet her.

Remembering he'd said he would be there in ten minutes, she snatched up her purse and her keys, and looked over her shoulder to find Chloe curled up in her now vacated seat on the sofa. "Have to go out for some underwear, Chloe! Keep that seat warm for me, sweetie!"

CHAPTER NINE

Sam was waiting for her in the lot outside of *Angelica's Delicate Secrets*, one hip indolently propped against his front fender and a whimsical smile on his lips, when Emma pulled up and got out of her car. He hadn't been sure she would come even though she had made out like she was there already but he was glad she had. He wanted to see her again, to talk to her about her ideas for the coffee shop.

He also wanted to ask a few questions about the research she had done. The information in the document she had given him would make for a great general interest book and he was hoping he could talk her into allowing him to put it into print. Right now, he envisioned placing copies on each of the tables at the One Shot—a bit of a conversation piece his customers could thumb through and talk about. A coffee table book was a super idea but he couldn't do a thing with it without Emma's permission.

If he were honest with himself, he would admit he wanted to kiss her again, too. And he *was* honest to a fault—usually—but this time he was a bit suspicious of what had happened the night she'd stopped by the shop after closing time and he was afraid whatever might be going on between him and Emma was happening because of the items they each had picked up at Seville's Antiques. Crazy as that sounded.

He blamed Jordan and Kaylee for making him wonder whether or not something supernatural was involved even though he found the whole idea of magically infused objects a little silly. No, it was downright ridiculous, actually. He didn't believe in magic. Power? Yes. Magic? No. He had his reasons for believing the way he did and none of them involved today's generally accepted rational motives of society.

But, according to Lindsay, something definitely huge and really powerful would have been the only thing to motivate Emma to kiss him before she got to know him —at least a little. He *was* barely more than a stranger, after all, and Lindsay had said it was very odd for her to have deviated from her normal behavior.

Of course Lindsay had tried to make it sound like he must be some super special guy but Sam knew he was just a regular ol' Joe. Or Sam, rather, but the point was he was no one special, unless you factored in his net worth. Emma hadn't seemed like the type of woman to make a move on a guy because of the size of his bank account, though. She was quiet, but he refused to believe she was scheming. She seemed shy and although he was a loud mouth most of the time who loved the company of other people, he found Emma's more modest traits adorable. It just *worked*—for her.

Couple her timidity with the intelligence he saw swimming in her gaze every time he'd looked into her eyes and you had a winning combination for inciting interest. Sam was definitely interested. Especially after their kiss. Or maybe he was interested in her in spite of it? The question had been driving him mad for days. He needed to know if he was drawn to her naturally, or if there was something supernatural—thanks to the Seville sisters—in play here.

Sam wanted his attraction to Emma to be natural.

He believed it was, too, and his curiosity where she was concerned was a thing which begged exploring but Emma was not being cooperative in the least. Three times he had asked Lindsay to have her call him and three times she had not. Had she thought his kisses bad then?

Oh, come on, Sammy, the voice in his head drawled in a tone loaded with sarcasm. *You barely know the girl. There's no need to let your ego get involved.*

His mental voice was right. Ego wasn't needed at all. Just some good old fashioned, straight up conversation was all it should take to clear up the "will she, won't she" conversation in his head. He needed to talk to Emma and if she hadn't called when she had, he would have found another way to get in touch with her.

As she made her way across the parking lot toward him, he could see she was going to pretend she was fine with precisely where they were meeting. But the tinge of high color on her cheek bones declared otherwise. Clearly, she was embarrassed by their current location, and despite his genuine effort to try, he couldn't seem to keep his lips from twitching.

He thought about teasing her for inviting the strange man she had spontaneously kissed to shop for under-wear just so he could watch her flush and squirm beneath his gaze but he had a feeling he might get a slap or worse for his effort. Instead, he said, "It only takes you thirty minutes to shop for sexy underwear? It always takes me at least a few hours."

Emma cocked one brow at a haughty angle and speared him with a look. "I don't think I needed to know your proclivity toward ladies underwear, really. Now what is it you need me to sign?"

Ignoring her attempt to get this meeting over so she could turn around and leave, he said, "I'll bet a rich, opulent blue is your color. A nice jewel tone, like the sea."

Refusing to allow herself to be drawn into such an intimate conversation with him, Emma hitched her bag higher on her shoulder. "And I'll bet I'm leaving again if we don't finish this soon. I've someone else waiting for me."

"Chloe, perhaps? Your foofy white cat?" Her blush

gave her away and he grinned. "Lindsay told me about her. Hey, looks like we have something besides memories in common! I have a cute little Husky myself, a pup named Jabez who likes to run. We should introduce them to each other someday."

The thought of doing anything with her after today made him feel surprisingly wistful. He knew he had to do something *now* or this was going to end badly—for both of them.

"You have some papers for me?"

Unable to draw her out of the shell of determined aloofness she'd retreated into, Sam finally reached through the open window of his car to collect a thick stack of papers which he flipped through before handing them over to her, his eyes lingering on her lips before he once more started to speak. "It's just standard percentages and a standard term but I'm willing to negotiate."

Without bothering to read the papers to see to what she was specifically agreeing, Emma clicked the end of the pen she'd brought with her from her car with her thumb, flipped through the pages directly to the one at the end and quickly signed her name before handing them back to him.

"There you go. You have my consent to use the research and drawings in whatever way you'd like. Now if you will excuse me, I really have to leave."

She turned to go but he caught her shoulder, halting her almost desperate flight. "Emma, wait."

Pausing, Emma turned to look back at him to see

what else he had to say, and immediately wished she hadn't.

"You've absolutely nothing to be embarrassed over or ashamed of, you know," he told her. "I very much wanted to kiss you, too—from the moment we crossed swords over that quilt in Seville's, I believe."

Don't do it, Emma. Don't listen to him. You're too emotionally eager right now to believe him. But, oh, did she want to believe. He had enjoyed the moment as much as she had? The warmth filling his eyes said he wouldn't mind doing it again, either, if only she would agree.

Making a slashing motion with her hand, she shook her head no and said, "Stop it, Sam. Just stop it, please. I know you can see that my cheeks are already on fire from inadvertently sending you here, and this—"

She had been about to say all this talk about kissing wasn't helping matters at all but he interrupted.

"Would it help if I admitted that I'm burning too, Emma? Just not anywhere you can see."

To think that Sam was burning with need for her made her suddenly go weak in the knees. Gasping in surprise at his admission, she again shook her head no. "I told you—kissing you that night was a mistake. A big one, mine, and so something I don't intend to repeat."

"Even if I'd like you to?" His gaze burned into hers and it was hard for her to remember she was supposed to just come here and sign his papers and leave. "Emma, what we shared was, well, better than nice, and it sure didn't feel like a mistake to me."

Turning away from the heated desire in his gaze, Emma started toward her car, muttering to herself every step of the way. "Oh, I don't understand any of this. What is going *on* with me?"

If she thought her actions were odd, there was no telling how strange to Sam she seemed. Suddenly it occurred to her that she didn't *want* him to think her strange. She'd barely made it to her car before she stopped and spun on one heel to stalk back to him and explain.

"Look, I'm sorry I let things get way out of control the other night but it was only because of those dreams."

Sam frowned. "What dreams?"

Emma was confused, then frustrated, then embarrassed and annoyed. "I—oh, never mind. I figured Lindsay would have told you by now, but ..." But obviously Lindsay hadn't and now Emma had no one to blame but herself for letting the cat out of the bag about her dreams. "Never mind. I—it's nothing really."

His expression told her he didn't believe her, but that he wasn't going to argue with her attempted apology—for now, at least it seemed. Crossing his arms over his chest, he leaned against his car again and nodded his acceptance of her explanation. "Alright, Emma. If you don't want to tell me that's your prerogative. It's fine. I'll pretend to be okay with your secrets if you'll promise to have dinner with me."

Dinner? Like the two of them together in close quarters? In a secluded space? "No, I—I can't."

He frowned down at her for a moment, then shrugged. "Then I want to know what you dreamed."

Not in a million years was Emma going to tell him what had happened in her dreams. Ignoring his stubborn stance and determined expression, she turned on a heel and headed for her car a second time—and her arms suddenly windmilled in the air as she was unexpectedly forced to fight for balance. Her feet had slipped on a patch of ice hidden in the shadow of a parked car and skated right out from under her!

"Woah! Easy there. I've got you." She felt a warm hand clasp tight around her upper arm and then she was curled against an even warmer body, enveloped by strong arms as her face nestled against a wide, firm chest.

Sam.

Burrowing her face deeper, she dragged in a slow breath, taking in his scent as she nestled—just for a second, she promised herself—closer to the man she had so often dreamed about. He smelled so good—like the sinfully hot fire of warm brandy and the pure spiky ice of cool mint.

Being in his arms again felt good, too.

The duality of the sensual experience was very much like the pleasure of walking into the blessed cool relief of a deep shade on a hot summer day or the slow spread of soothing heat on a frigid winter afternoon—the kind that climbed upward from one's toes, permeating through skin and muscle and bone until the entirety of your body was infused with the relaxing comfort of warmth.

Her fingers itched to clench and furl into his skin much the way she'd seen Chloe knead the quilt she'd purchased from the antique store and her mouth yearned to feel the silky glide of his lips on hers once more.

"I'm not dreaming," she whispered to remind herself she was currently wide awake and very much in a public place at the moment and should not give in to the wicked temptations currently firing her blood. The sound of her own voice so breathless and her words so throaty, filled as they were with the urgency of desire now thrumming through her entire body, snapped Emma out of the contented languor she'd fallen into and she jerked upright, pulling quickly out of his embrace. "I—thank you for saving me. I have to go now."

Without meeting his gaze, she turned and walked away—carefully avoiding the ice this time—and he did not try to stop her. His voice, however, carried across the lot just as her hand touched the door, his words making her pause. "It was my pleasure, Emma."

Flushed and still far too warm, she got into the car and quickly started the engine because she knew if she didn't leave right now she might be tempted to let him know the pleasure had not been entirely his.

"Gem told me you'd gone to meet with Emma Riley to get her to sign those contracts." Jordan spoke while he worked, his entire attention focused on the antique *chiffonier* in front of him. "Did you ask her out?"

"Didn't get a chance," Sam told him. "I don't think there will be one, either. Emma Riley doesn't actually like me for some reason."

Jordan peered at him over the edge of the door he was sanding. "Everybody likes you."

"Not Emma." Sam walked over to the table where Jordan had various bits and pieces of the cabinet laid out for sanding before he started applying the many layers of stain and then a glossy finish. "Hand me a scrap of that sandpaper and I'll help."

"There's some one-twenty grit on the workbench. I'm

about done with this go around. You can start on the next."

Sam found the sandpaper easily enough and joined Jordan at the table. "Does it matter which piece I start on?"

Jordan pointed. "Do that one first. I'll finish this and then come around to start on the one beside it. Did she sign the papers or not?"

"She signed them." Which was what Sam wanted, but at the same time, the way she had signed them was cause for concern. It was bugging him. "Signed every line, but she didn't read the first word of it, and that almost makes me wish I'd taken them back before she had a chance."

"Hm. Why would you want to do that?"

Sam could tell Jordan was only half paying attention to what he was saying, distracted as he was with the project in front of him, so he bent to the shelf in front of him to put in a little elbow grease of his own. As he moved the sandpaper back and forth across the wood, he asked himself the same question. Why did he wish he'd taken them back? He'd gotten what he wanted. Wasn't that good enough?

He shrugged. "Something seems off about it. Emma didn't strike me as the kind of person who would sign something she hadn't read. I mean, think about it. Seriously. What business owner do you know who would sign something as insignificant as a memo they hadn't read, much less a contract."

"Business owner?" Jordan murmured as if those were the only two words he had heard. "What does she do?"

"Freelancer. Research specialist from what I hear and if that isn't her official designation, it should be. She's good. Freelancers use contracts. She should have read mine."

"Is this going to bug you until doomsday?" Jordan paused to ask. "If it is, call her."

Sam shook his head. "I don't think so, man."

"Why not?"

Sam felt his brow furrow, and hiked up his shoulder in a half shrug. "There's this whole on again off again thing going on with her. As long as I've got my arms around her, she seems to like me fine. But the minute there's space enough between us to breathe, she does everything she can to get away from me as quickly as possible—like signing a contract she hasn't read."

"Well there's your solution!" Jordan grinned. "Keep your arms around her, man."

Sam couldn't hold back a chuckle but still he shook his head. "She doesn't want *that*, either."

Somehow, he had gained Jordan's full attention during the past five minutes because when he looked up, Jordan was staring quizzically at him through narrowed eyelids. The intensity of his stare made Sam uneasy. "What?"

"You could always shred the contract and forget about the book."

Sam knew he could, but he didn't want to. He wanted

that book for the One Shot and even though he wasn't exactly sure why it was so important to him, he wanted Emma's name to be on it as author. He gave Jordan a rueful look. "Fine. I'll call her. Right after we finish this round of sanding."

As it turned out, he didn't have to. Just as he was locking away the last of the tools, his cell phone rang.

"Sam speaking," he answered without bothering to look at the screen. It was after hours for the coffee shop so whoever was calling expected him to answer anyway.

"What did I sign?"

Emma's voice came as a pleasant surprise. Waving to Jordan, Sam motioned to his phone and pointed toward the house in a sort of gesticulated man speak for "You go ahead. I'm going to take this call then go home for the night."

Jordan nodded and a few seconds later, Sam heard his truck fire up.

"A contract," he offered vaguely as he collected his coat and shut off the lights. "I wondered if you would break down and call or if I would have to call you."

"What kind of contract?" she asked, ignoring his attempt at semi-pleasant banter.

"Pre-nup," Sam blurted without thinking. Teasing people was almost second nature to him and it was no different with Emma. It didn't occur to him until after he'd ran his mouth that doing so might not be the best way for him to move forward with Emma.

Still, if he was in for a penny he might as well be in

for a pound, or that was what his grandmother used to say. After a quick, mental shrug, he said, "And a marriage contract. We're as good as honeymooners, darling."

Then he rolled his eyes in regret over what he'd said.

She was going to hang up on him. Climbing into his truck, he closed the door and started the engine while waiting for her to end the call, which he actually figured she would do rather than offer a biting retort of one sort or the other.

Instead, she asked, "Do I get a copy?"

Sam wondered if she'd heard a word he'd said. "Sure. I'll need your address but I can't get to a pen and paper right now. Give me a minute to get inside the house."

It was only a short drive from the workshop to the house. As a matter of fact, he could have walked, but when he'd got there this afternoon and saw Jordan parked at the shop, he just drove over instead of parking at the house and walking.

"I'll just come by the One Shot tomorrow and pick it up if that's okay?" There was an edge to her voice that smacked of discomfort. Was she uncomfortable with everybody or was her tentative reserve only for him?

"I'll be there. Early or afternoon?"

"Early. I need to visit the library and pick up a couple reference books anyway so I will stop by the cafe on my way in." She paused. "You don't have to personally hand over the papers. I'm perfectly fine with picking them up from your barista, or whoever is available."

"I'll be available. It's not a problem, Emma," Sam told

her. "I'll see you in the morning."

She ended the call and Sam grinned over the little thrill of anticipation he felt about her upcoming visit. He could show her the architect's drawings he'd commissioned from her sketches and maybe she would even answer a few questions he had about preferred placement, orientation, and such.

For some reason, from the minute she'd dropped off the research and done those drawings, Sam felt Emma had become integral to his plans for redesigning the look and feel of the One Shot. She had good ideas and he believed he could trust her opinions—at least in regard to the Coffee Cozies and Latte Lounges. Those little outdoor nooks had been her idea and he thought it only fair she have a chance to offer more in-depth input on how they were placed and utilized.

"*Arf!*"

Jabez met him at the front door and Sam bent to give his fur a ruffle.

"Hey! Hey there, boy! Guess what? Emma's coming by the One Shot tomorrow. Do you think I should dress up for the occasion?"

"*Arf, arf!*"

Sam laughed.

"Yeah, you're right. I wouldn't want to make the customers uncomfortable by showing up in a tux!" He headed for the kitchen, enjoying the comforting *click, click, click* of Jabez's toenails on the hardwood floor as the dog followed him through the house.

Opening the fridge, he took out the half gallon of milk and opened the top before raising it to drink straight from the jug, half tensing in anticipation as he did so. If Grandma Ellie were still alive, she would have blistered his ears with a scolding for such bad manners. With only Jabez to see what he'd done, there was nothing to worry about.

A touch of wistful sadness drifted over him like one of his grandma's quilts and he sighed, suddenly grateful for the Husky's presence. "Thanks for the warm and enthusiastic greeting, old boy. It sure is nice to have someone waiting who is actually glad to see me when I come home."

~

EMMA WRAPPED her coat tighter and hurried toward the front entrance of the One Shot Coffee Cafe. The weather report promised Hawthorne Grove would see sun today but right now it was still too early and too cold.

A blast of toasty warmth hit her full on as soon as she stepped inside the cafe. Blinking, she lifted her head and looked toward the bar, hoping to find only the barista waiting but knowing Sam would be there instead. She was right.

"Good morning, Miss Riley," Gem greeted. "Caramel crème latte? Hard mint cocoa? What can I get you this morning?"

"I'll take care of it, Gem," Sam interrupted, his eyes

surveying her from top to toe while he pulled a mug from beneath the counter and began filling it with something hot and chocolaty. "Good morning, Emma."

"Good morning to the both of you," she said, nodding to Gem. Turning to Sam, she asked, "Do you have the papers?"

"They're in my office in the back. Here," he said, handing her the mug. "Sip on this. It'll warm you up while I go get them."

Ignoring the sounds of early morning coffee drinkers who were already seated at one of several tables, sipping at mugs of warm caffeine rich sustenance, Emma opted to sit at the bar. Slipping off her gloves, she wrapped her half frozen fingers around the cup Sam had offered and sighed with pleasure while she waited for Sam.

A few minutes later, he laid a stack of legal sized papers in front of her that had been stapled together on one corner. "Thanks."

"Like I told you yesterday, everything's pretty standard but you should let me know if there's anything you don't agree with and I will amend it immediately." He laid another page in front of her, and Emma's eyes widened before snapping up to stare at him in confusion.

"You're in luck," he told her. "When I went to get your copy of the contract, the designer had faxed over a concept for the cover. What do you think?"

Emma didn't quite know what to think but she was looking at a picture of a book—the kind you'd find on a table in a lounge or lobby or an upscale living room coffee table. What had her tongue-tied was the author's name. It was hers! But...

Sliding the cover concept to the side, she picked up the contract—a publishing contract—looking for the name of the publisher. She figured Sam had his own and that was why he was able to get the whole package of a book deal together so quickly. Either that, or he'd paid a vanity publisher to do it up for him. She was wrong. The name on the top of the contract was a well-known and well respected publishing house.

"How?" Her gaze had returned to search his. "Isn't there a protocol or a process for getting published? Don't answer that. I know there is and I know it generally takes months to hear back from them. How did you manage this so quickly?"

"The editor is a friend of mine. When I told her what I had and what I wanted to do, she asked to look at your research. I faxed it over and the next day she faxed me the contract."

"But you can't—this--this isn't something you did to sell more coffee, Sam. This is a real publishing deal. If I can believe what I'm reading, they want to turn my research into a book and sell it." Emma suddenly felt overwhelmed. "Did you already send the signed copy of this back to your friend?"

Sam's expression clouded and he shook his head. "While I would love to say yes because I can sense your need to put a halt to this right now, no I haven't. I want to, but I couldn't send over a contract you'd signed without having read."

Relief washed through her. "Thank you. I appreciate that."

"Unlike the bit where I helped you get a publishing contract, I take it?" One corner of his lips turned wryly upward.

"No," Emma was distracted by the million and one thoughts suddenly spinning through her head. "I actually appreciate that, too. It's just—"

She studied him, uncertain what to make of a man who submitted her work to a publisher but then held off sending back the signed contract because he knew she hadn't read it. He was presumptuous and, well, genuinely *nice*.

"I haven't thought of publishing my work for a while now. I'd given up on the idea, to be honest. But you made it so easy and—" She broke off and looked away from the gleam of satisfaction for having done something great for her in his eyes. "I would never have submitted the research I did for you to a publisher as a book. What made you do it?"

"The coffee service." He shrugged and walked over to the register to check out a customer. After a few words and a wave goodbye, he came back to pick up their conversation. "Every time I looked at it, your paper was in my thoughts. There's a human interest element in your title a mile wide and I really think my customers will enjoy reading it."

Emma heard what he said. It made sense, too. But she couldn't get past the idea that if she only allowed him to return the contract, she would be a published author. Just like that. With a simple fax, she would step out of the shadows of research grunt and into the limelight of recognition for her work in the form of having her own name on the cover of a book. A real book that Sam and the publisher who had sent the contract believed people would want to buy. "Wow."

Sam's chuckle brought her out of her musings. Almost instantly, she was plunged into a whirlpool of unease even as she stared at the mock up of the book —*her* book—in awe. The publishing company might require things of her to help promote the book that she wasn't prepared to give or do—like appear on a radio talk show or maybe even local TV. *Oh, no.*

"I can't!" Really. She couldn't. The mere thought made her nauseated. And yet, at the same time, something inside her unfurled—something wondrous and glad and yes, filled with a sense of pride.

Her entire family would look at her in a whole new light to see her name on the cover of a book like the one in the picture she was having a hard time looking away from. For once, she would fit in. At last, she would measure up. In the eyes of her family, she would suddenly be good enough.

Glancing at Sam again to make sure he hadn't noticed how the lump of emotion swelling in her throat made her eyes go all watery, she searched his face for—something. Courage? Motivation? Support? To her surprise, she found all three in waiting for her.

"You *can* do this, Emma. I'll help. If you run into a challenge, let me know and I'll help you work it out," he promised. Though she found it surprising, she realized he meant it. "Your work is superb. You deserve to be recognized for it."

Well, that put roses in her cheeks—and warmth in her heart. Coming from him, the compliment seemed so much more meaningful although she wasn't sure why. For reasons she really didn't understand at the moment, she nodded. "All right. I will."

His grin was worth the concession. Not to mention it set off all sorts of happy fireworks inside her when he turned the full measure of it on her.

"Atta girl!" he cheered. "And now that you've made the decision to go ahead with it, you should celebrate. Call your family. Call Lindsay and the rest of your friends. Heck, if you want, you can have them all come here. I know a caterer—"

"No," she said, cutting him off. Somehow the idea of sharing her news with the rest of the world didn't seem comfortable. But Sam...

"I'd rather have a nice, quiet dinner at home." Peeking up at him from behind her lashes, she asked, "Would you care to share it with me?"

Something flashed in his eyes alongside the subdued happiness she saw. He nodded. "Absolutely."

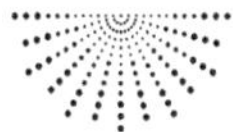

CHAPTER ELEVEN

*E*mma's hands were still shaking when she pulled up in front of the grocery store. What in the world had she been thinking? She still couldn't believe she had invited Sam to have dinner with her. One minute she had been thinking logically and rationally, and the next, she'd let her stupid mouth ramble out that stupid invitation. Now she not only had to cook she also had to smile and be a gracious host for however long it took them to eat dinner.

"Why, why, *why* did I open my mouth?" Reaching into her purse, she took out her phone. She would call Lindsay. Lindsay would know what to do. She would help her figure out how to cancel tonight's dinner with Sam without looking like a total jerk.

Before she could press the little phone icon, something made her hesitate. Did she even want Lindsay to know about what had happened between her and Sam?

In her mind, the conversation played out. "I dropped off some research at the One Stop, Sam kissed me. I met him at the lingerie shop where I signed a contract without reading it. Then I had to call Sam and find out what the contract had been about..."

Emma could easily imagine Lindsay's wide eyes, her dropped jaw, and the million and one questions that would inevitably follow. Lindsay Vale had a curious streak a mile wide and Emma knew she would not stop needling until Emma spilled every detail—even the bits where she would have to admit to being interested in Sam. No, she decided. Best to leave Lindsay out of it. But she mentally weighed the pros and cons of her invitation even after she got home with the ingredients she'd needed to make dinner.

Glancing around the bag she was carrying, Emma heeled the door shut behind her and bent to put her purse and keys on the table by the door. She hoped Sam's tastes weren't too refined because the only thing she could think of to cook for the two of them was a simple meal of *steak au poivre* with mustard sauce, baby potatoes, and brussel sprouts.

"*Meow.*"

"Hi, Chloe. Did you miss me?" Leaning sideways to put the bags on the table, Emma bent to scratch the spot on top of Chloe's head between her ears, and started to apologize for being late. "Sorry it took so long. After I stopped by the One Shot to pick up the contract from Sam, I had to go by the grocer for steak and veggies. Can you believe what I did? You'll never believe it. I asked Sam to come over here for dinner. With me. Genius, right?"

The cat twitched her tail and stared up at her in silence while Emma busied herself with emptying the bags and putting away food.

Finished, Emma propped her hands on her hips and blew a stray curl out of her eyes. "I don't know what I was thinking. I *wasn't* thinking!" she corrected. "If I had been, then none of this dinner business would have been necessary."

Chloe cocked her head to one side, peering up at her mistress. "*Meow.*"

Emma huffed out a sigh and bent to scoop the cat into her arms. "I know. I know. You're only interested until I put out your food, right?"

Lying contentedly in the crook of Emma's arm, Chloe purred while Emma went to the pantry to collect her food, chattering on to the cat about the coming dinner engagement as she did so.

"What am I supposed to do for the half hour or so it takes us to get through dinner, Chloe?" she asked the feline. Depositing the cat on the floor, she opened the cat food tin and grabbed a spoon to dish half of it into the cat's bowl. "I don't talk to people. I'm not a conversationalist. I'm a—a watcher. An observer of others who actually have a life. Unlike me."

Chloe glanced up at her once and then promptly ignored her in favor of the meal awaiting in her dish.

"What if I burn something? What if I can't think of anything to say to him once he gets here?" Emma continued, completely disregarding her pet's current inattention. "Or worse, what happens if I forget this is the *real* Sam again, not the Sam from my dreams, and I let him kiss me? Or I kiss him?"

Her gaze drifted back to Chloe, who had finished her own dinner, and sat quietly grooming her fur while her owner indulged in a momentary mental meltdown. "It's days like these when I really do wish I believed in magic, Chloe. I could really use a confidence spell or two right now."

The cat got up, shook once, and padded over to the bedroom door. "*Meow.*"

Emma arched a brow. "Really? I suppose you've forgotten what happens every time I touch that quilt."

"Meow," the cat said again, and Emma made a quick decision before she had too much time to think about it.

"Okay, fine. I'll try it, but after I get dinner going. I'm warning you, though, if it looks stupid, you'll have to come up with something else in a hurry. I have a feeling Sam Huntingdon is the kind of man who is never late."

Chloe sat back on her haunches and flicked an ear.

Emma laughed and spun toward the kitchen. "Wow. I can't believe I'm discussing this with my cat—as if you could really help me feel better about being alone with a man I've barely met. I can't believe it even matters."

In the kitchen, she took out a casserole dish and went to the fridge for the steak and mustard. The meat would need to marinate for a bit and she had just enough time if she started right now.

"Sam is just a guy I'm having dinner with. There's no reason to try and impress him, right?" Realizing she was talking to the cat again, she she shook her head. Muttering under her breath, she went to dig a spoon out from the drawer for the mustard. "Right."

~

CHAMPAGNE IN HAND, Sam looked up at the row of two-story townhouse apartments lining the street where Emma Riley lived and realized he actually felt a little nervous about having dinner with her tonight.

His brows rose at the realization. Being out of his element felt odd. He'd always just seemed to fit into any scenario or situation, except when it came to *Emma*. With her, there was a quiet whisper of caution in the back of his mind telling him to be careful or he would mess things up. The same voice promised if he did that Emma would probably never want to see him again.

Tread lightly, tread lightly, he repeated to himself, letting the words play rhythmically in his head in perfect sync with the sound of his footsteps on the stairs as he made his way up to the entrance of her apartment.

Tonight's invitation to dinner had not been easily won. He was well aware Emma had invited him only because she thought she owed him something for winning a book deal for her, but Sam didn't care. A thank-you dinner was as good a reason as any if it allowed him to see her again.

"You're early," Emma said from the now open door of her apartment. She'd opened the door in front of him before he could raise his hand to knock. Sam glanced at his watch, then back at her, and grinned.

"Five minutes. Which means I'm right on time. The champagne can chill a bit more before we pop the cork to celebrate."

"You brought champagne?" Taking the bottle of *Krug Clos d'Ambonnay* from him, she motioned for him to follow her inside, then read the label on her way to the kitchen.

Sam followed, his eyes taking in the way her bright hair flowed over one shoulder across the soft, buttery colored sweater she wore before focusing on the swing of her lemon yellow bohemian skirt while he tried to remember this wasn't a *date*. Emma had not dressed up for him, he reminded himself, but he was still secretly thrilled to see her in an outfit that didn't hide every one of her womanly assets from view for whatever reason she'd chosen to wear it.

"You weren't supposed to bring anything," Emma grumped good-naturedly as he followed her deeper into the apartment. "You already did your part with the contract. Dinner was supposed to be all me."

Sam's thoughts took an unexpected stroll on the naughty side and he almost choked on the sudden urge to laugh out loud at her clearly unintended double *entendre.* He knew she hadn't meant what she's said the way it sounded. If she had, his reaction would have been far different. Still, his brows rose and he tilted his head to indicate the bottle she held.

"If that's the case, maybe you'd better leave that out," he said, his lips working in a vain attempt to hold back his chuckles. "Wouldn't want you to get a chill."

"Wow. You brought a two thousand dollars a bottle champagne and we're having simple *steak au poivre* with potatoes and brussel sprouts." Glancing up in confusion as if she'd just realized he'd said something, she said, "Wait, what?"

"Never mind," Sam told her, waving away his comment as unimportant. "I love *steak au poivre* and the champagne is perfect for the occasion. We are celebrating, remember?"

"Right, although I still can hardly believe it." After a quick shake of her head to bring her back to the present, she pointed through the arched doorway leading off the smallish galley kitchen before opening an overhead cabinet.

"Dinner is in there," she said over her shoulder as she selected a matched pair of glasses for the champagne.

Sam noted they were made of the finest cut crystal, and when he walked into the dining nook, he couldn't help but be impressed by the selection of elegant dinnerware and silver service she'd laid out for their meal. "Wow. Is this how you normally have a quiet dinner at home, or did you do all this for me?"

Joining him in the nook, she shrugged. It's usually just me and Chloe and I tend to favor the *Chinet* but as you've mentioned, we are celebrating."

Gaining a new appreciation for the woman who leaned over to set the glasses she'd brought onto the table beside each of their place settings, Sam nodded in understanding. Still, he couldn't help but stare quizzically at her when she came back from the kitchen with their plates and took her seat across from him. Emma Riley clearly had refined tastes—something he hadn't expected though he did wholeheartedly approve.

"Something wrong?" she asked, noting his curious expression.

"No, not at all." Forcing himself to pay attention now to dinner rather than the intriguing woman who was sharing it, Sam picked up his fork and knife to try the steak. It was the perfect temperature and so tender it practically melted on his tongue. He took a minute to savor the flavors of pepper and mustard sauce before slicing off another bite. "Mm. This is delicious, Emma. Maybe in addition to writing books you should open a restaurant."

Glancing up, he noted the sudden blush on her cheeks. She ducked her head and concentrated on cutting her own portion. "You certainly are good at making a girl feel accomplished."

"You *are* accomplished. You were already a fantastic researcher and writer before I came along. I didn't have anything to do with that."

"I don't know about fantastic—" she broke off. "Still, I would never have thought to submit that particular piece to a publisher and I have you to thank for the resulting contract."

"And so you have, with this delicious dinner. I appreciate that you offered to share it with me. I had hoped we might—" He broke off to consider his words. Motioning to the meal in front of him, he said, "I want you to know you didn't have to do this to repay me for anything, Emma. Other than hoping to be given the opportunity to share what you had learned with my customers, I didn't expect to get anything out of what I did."

Leaning back in his chair, one side of his lips curled wryly upward, he said, "Well, other than a chance to see you again, that is."

Cocking her head to one side, Emma peered curiously across the table at him. "Why *did* you want to see me again?"

Sam knew he needed to think his answer through if he didn't want tonight to be the last time he saw her, but found himself blurting, "You intrigue me. I'll even admit I was curiously enchanted with you from the first time I laid eyes on you in the antique store."

"Enchanted. Right," Emma said with a slow roll of her eyes.

She didn't believe him but for some inexplicable reason, it was suddenly very important to Sam that she did. Completely serious now, he leaned forward and said, "Emma—I *like* you. You're a beautiful woman with a lot of talent, likely in more areas than I've had time to discover. You're passionate, too, although you probably don't like to admit that. You're obviously careful about getting involved with anyone. And particular."

When she said nothing, only continued to stare at him as if she couldn't possibly believe anything he was saying, he said, "I see hints of deep intelligence in those gorgeous, coffee colored eyes when I look at you, and to be honest, I am actually a little terrified you are just way too sharp for a guy like me."

Afraid he'd said too much already, Sam told himself to stop, to wait for her to respond. But words continued to spill from his lips, words he needed to get said before she called foul on his attempts to impress the truth of his interest in her. "The combination of all those things showing up—all qualities I admire—packs quite a wallop for a guy like me. All I get to see is a whole lot of medi-ocre most days."

He shrugged and picked up his knife and fork again to slice another portion of steak. "I'm sorry if you find my intrigue strange, but all of those things I've mentioned stir up a crazy sort of need in me to find out what else you might be hiding behind those impossibly long lashes of yours."

Blinking said lashes to break the direct contact of their gazes, she lowered her eyes to stare quietly at her plate rather than meet his eyes and Sam sighed. "My only *ulterior motive,* if I even have one, Emma, is that I would like to get to know you better. Is that so hard for you to accept? Or is it that I am really that distasteful a person to you?"

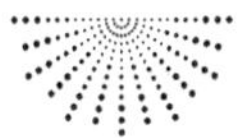

CHAPTER TWELVE

*E*mma wanted to melt into a puddle in her chair and drip down onto the floor, out of his direct line of sight. Everything he'd said, all those *nice* things he'd said about her, couldn't possibly be the truth, even if she wanted them to be. Using the quilt for a tablecloth had been a terrible idea. Touching the thing wasn't just affecting her—it was obviously affecting Sam, too.

Casting an accusatory glance in Chloe's direction, Emma tried to find her tongue. "I—I don't find you distasteful at all."

She didn't. Not only was he easily the most handsome man she'd seen in a while, he was easy to talk with, listen to, easy to be with, and most of all, easy to want more from. Especially when one dreamed about him every night. The scary part was how much she was enjoying his company, his presence, right now.

Night after night, she had dreamed of him and after

she woke, she'd thought about what she had dreamed until it was time to sleep again. Tonight, being with him like this over a quiet dinner in her apartment, it was like he'd never left and she liked him being there. In her home. In her life.

The realization jolted her. "Sam? What are we doing here? Not *here*, in my apartment, but here … together? You and I, we don't, this isn't..."

"Magic," Sam finished for her. Gesturing toward the table, he said, "Jordan and his fiancee, Kaylee, would swear it's the quilt you picked up at Sevilles, but I don't believe it is. Our attraction, the things we feel for each other, they're real, Emma."

Emma's eyes widened and she leaned away from the table so she wouldn't be touching the material. "The quilt? What about the quilt?"

Humor flashed in his eyes and he chuckled. "Kaylee believes the Seville sisters possess supernatural powers, that they are somehow able to infuse objects from their store with magical abilities—like the ability to bring two people together."

That would explain the dreams, she thought. Her interest more than piqued, she leaned forward again. "Did she buy something from Sevilles, too?"

Sam nodded. "A snow globe. Inside was a house that she swore was a tiny replica of Jordan's place. She even admitted to seeing his dog in that thing once."

Emma's brows rose but she said, "Why would she

think it possessed magic? Just because there was a house and a dog inside doesn't mean..."

"Every time she looked at it, she thought of Jordan— to the point of distraction, apparently, because now she gives the thing credit for bringing the two of them together." He gave her a look. "Silly, huh?"

Her head cocked to one side, Emma ignored his question to ask one of her own. "What about her fiance? Did he buy something from the sisters as well?"

"Jordan?" Sam nodded. "A letter box. He found a dog tag inside. To hear him tell the story, that little metal tag led him to the shelter where Kaylee volunteers. They promptly fell in love and the rest is history."

Peering at him curiously, she tried to wrap her mind around the concept of something outside her realm of experience pulling her and Sam together. She could certainly feel a pull, but Sam ...

"You don't believe in magic?"

"Do you?" he countered, and though she wished she could give her imagination up to something so flighty, she could not.

Emma shook her head and confessed, "No."

"But you do believe there is a connection between us, don't you?" He smiled at her and she felt her entire body quiver. "Don't bother trying to lie about it, Emma. I can see it in your eyes even when your lips say otherwise."

Pushing her chair back from the table, Emma said, "I'm not sure. I mean, I didn't even know you existed before Sevilles, and then..."

"I took on a starring role in your midnight fantasies?" Sam teased with a comical waggle of his brows, and Emma felt her cheeks burn.

It was true—he had featured in her dreams quite a few times—enough to leave her sleep deprived and frustrated to be sure. "I'm not sure what is real."

"Hey, come on," Sam cajoled, pushing his own chair back. "You just told me you don't believe in magic, right? Here, give me your hand."

Reaching across the table, she did, and he laced his fingers with hers. "See? Flesh and blood. Skin and bone. I'm no dream, Emma, but it fascinates me to no end to know I've been in yours."

His eyes had gone dark and his voice had that low, husky quality she remembered from her dreams. Heat spiked through her and her pulse slowed as bits and pieces of the fantasies he'd joked about starring in flitted through her mind.

Snatching her hand away, she said, "You stole my puzzle piece."

"True. But how else was I supposed to find you again? Trading my card for a piece of your puzzle was the only thing I could think of at the time." He arched a brow. "One of the sisters called me out on it after you left, you know. It was cute how she all but demanded I do the honorable thing and return what I had stolen from you."

"You haven't returned it," Emma reminded him and to her surprise she saw the hint of a flush on his cheekbones. It was adorable. She grinned.

"What? Okay, so I still have the piece, but I always intended to give it back to you."

"When?"

"At first, I planned to trade it for the quilt." He shrugged and leaned back in his chair again, putting more space between them. Emma physically felt his withdrawal. It was like someone had peeled away her coat, leaving her outside in the cold. She shivered.

"Why are you so obsessed with the thing? It's just a cover, after all."

His eyes met hers and Emma thought she saw a flicker of sadness in his. "It reminds me of my grandmother."

"She must have been a very special lady to have such an effect on you."

Sam nodded. "She was."

Curious, Emma picked up her fork and said, "Tell me about her."

Half an hour passed, then another as Sam regaled her with tales of his childhood. Dinner finished, they'd moved to the living room and now sat together on her sofa where Emma laughed while Sam regaled her with tales of some of the particularly boyish antics he had plagued his grandmother with.

"You were a terrible child," she pronounced finally, but he only laughed.

"Grandma Ellie never thought so. I was the light of her life, and she mine for most of my childhood." There was that flickering of something in his eyes again, and he grew quiet.

"You miss her," Emma pronounced and Sam instantly agreed.

"Grandma Ellie was my rock, a solid presence in a life that moved by like a whirlwind."

The emotion shining in his gaze was powerful. Emma swallowed hard. "You can have the quilt, Sam. I intended to give it to you weeks ago."

"Is that a subtle hint that you'd like me to help you clear the table now?" he teased.

Emma laughed. "No, but if you want to help, I won't refuse the offer."

Together, they moved back to the dining room to collect the dishes, still chattering on as they carried them through to the sink in the kitchen.

"You wash, I'll dry," Sam told her, taking up a terry weave towel from the counter. "And you can tell me about you. Where did you learn to draw? The sketches you did for the outdoor additions at the One Shot were very professional."

Emma flushed at his praise.

"My brother taught me. Well, harassed me into learning would be more accurate," she admitted. "I had this idea to start my own furniture production business, you see, where my company would fabricate the most intricate designs on the planet. But whenever I attempted to describe something to him, he would say, 'Show me.' Then he would completely ignore me and anything I tried to say until I was able to sketch a complete concept for him."

Surprised, Sam said, "Furniture? Really?"

"Baroque. It is such a feminine style and at the time I had my head way up in the clouds."

Sam took the plate she handed him and dried it. "You? No way. I can't imagine you working a blank on a lathe with a shaping tool or dreaming about furniture in general, even if it is girly. Maybe you better explain what you mean by 'head in the clouds'?"

Emma shrugged. "I guess you could say I was a dreamer. I thought I could carve out a fairy tale, drape it with filmy gauze, and make a million dollars from it. But dreams, as you obviously know, aren't practical. Hard work gets you what you want. Ideas and sketches? Those are just fanciful notions on paper."

Old hurt zipped through her and she looked away, focusing on the silverware she was washing instead of his reaction but out of the corner of her eye she saw him arch a brow.

"Those are called project concepts and blueprints where I come from, Emma. I've paid thousands of dollars for hastily drawn ideas and quick sketches—a few of which were mapped out on the back of a stained napkin over a rushed lunch."

"My father hasn't." She dropped the casserole dish she'd used to marinate their steak into the water and mimicked the voice she had heard so often. "Drawings?

Bah! Show me something concrete I can reach out and touch and I'll think about it!"

"He wanted a prototype?"

Emma made a face. "He wanted me to stop dreaming and do something practical with my life."

"Ah. Practical. That explains it," Sam said, and Emma turned to him with a questioning look.

"Explains what?"

With one finger, he reached out and traced a line from her temple to her chin. "Why your mouth says you don't believe in magic while your eyes brim with an unforgettable hope someone will prove it exists."

Tears pricked her eyelids. With a single sentence, he had summed up the last seven years of her life. Why did he have to make it sound so possible? "Sam, I—"

He cut off her words with a kiss.

One minute he was standing there drying a casserole dish as if it were the most normal thing in the world for a billionaire business owner like himself to do, and the next, he was enfolding her in his arms, his mouth crushed to hers.

His fingers threaded into her hair, holding her for his kiss, and Emma moaned her pleasure at his touch against his lips even as her own fingers slid over his shoulders and down the hard planes of his back to his hips.

This, she thought. This was what she had believed in all those years ago. Sam's kiss was powerful magic and epic fantasy, ultimate sin and utter bliss all rolled into one and she wanted more of it. So much more.

Giving herself over to the kiss, Emma forgot about the past, forgot about the contract, the book, her father—everything but Sam and the wonderful things he was making her feel. Time stood still, holding the two of them suspended in a moment of passion and wonder and bliss that was so far removed from what she'd felt in her dreams, Emma wondered if she'd died and found Heaven right there in his arms.

"*Mrrrweaooow!*"

The sudden, drawn out and miserable caterwauling at her ankles jerked Emma out of Sam's embrace. Eyes wide in fright, one hand clutched to her chest, she glared down at the cat and scolded. "Chloe! Good heavens, girl, you scared the *bejesus* out of me! What's wrong? Why are you bawling like that?"

Sam pushed Emma quickly behind him, his eyes scanning what he could see of her apartment from the kitchen while Emma bent and scooped the cat up, running her hands in soothing motions over her thick, fluffy white fur. The cat purred contentedly now that she was the focus of Emma's attention, and Emma laughed. "Oh, wow. You're actually jealous!"

"I think I am," Sam said, his expression completely serious. "But I hate to admit feeling envious of a cat."

"Wha—?" Emma burst out laughing. "I was talking about *Chloe,* you doof. She's fine now that she's in my arms and..."

"And you're no longer in mine, right?" Sam grinned. "I can assure you, she has every reason to feel that way.

There is a lot to be said about having your arms wrapped around a body. When you turn off those voices in your head constantly urging you to caution, you melt like snow in an oven."

Emma buried her face in Chloe's fur to hide her blush. "Your arms being the oven in question," she dared. "Kissing you is like eating fire. I burn but I never want to escape the flames."

Sam's groan reverberated through her an instant before she felt his hands come around her waist from behind, pulling her against his hard frame while his lips sought out the sensitive skin of her nape.

He nibbled and she shivered, melting into him, but Chloe had other ideas. Hissing, she twisted in Emma's arms and swiped at Sam, batting him away from her mistress. Shocked, Emma scolded the furious feline and put her on the floor before turning to Sam to see what damage she had wrought.

Sam had a hand to his cheek, a wry grin turning his lips upward. "I guess we know what your cat thinks of us, huh?"

Emma reached up and pulled his fingers away. She gasped at the red streak Chloe's claws had left behind. "You're bleeding!"

"Only a little." Sam leaned in for another quick kiss but Emma ducked out of his reach.

"Let me clean that. I have some antiseptic spray here somewhere," she told him. She rummaged through drawers and opened cabinets.

"I've got it." Taking a piece of paper towel from the roll on her counter, he pressed it to the scratch, drying up the blood. "It's fine, Emma."

Turning, she glared at the cat. "I'm sorry. I don't know what got into her."

"I think that was her way of saying it is time for me to go." Sam muttered, then said, "I guess she's right. It is getting late, but I don't want to leave until you promise I'll see you again."

Casting a jaundiced eye at the cat, he said, "Next time at my place?"

Emma was immediately hesitant. "Sam, I don't think—"

"Don't. Think. Just say yes. You can even bring Chloe with you if you want. We can introduce her to Jabez. Say yes, Emma. Otherwise, I'll have to keep the last piece of your puzzle forever," he teased, but there was such appeal in his gaze, Emma couldn't find the words to turn him down. She didn't want to, anyway, although she knew she probably should. Sam Huntingdon was not the kind of man she needed to get involved with.

"Alright. Yes, I'll come."

Sam's relief was visible. He grinned. "Great. I'll call you tomorrow with my address and we'll do dinner at around seven. That okay?"

"It's perfect," Emma told him as she walked with him to the door. "Thank you again, Sam, for what you did with the book."

"Don't mention it. Thank you, for dinner."

She nodded, and opened the door for him. "Good-night, Sam."

He paused in the doorway and leaned in for another kiss, this one light and gentle. When he lifted his head, Emma thought she might just fall at his feet in a gooey puddle. He smiled.

"Goodnight, Emma," he murmured before he turned and hurried down the steps.

Emma slowly closed the door behind him. Turning the lock, she leaned against the door, feeling the loneliness pushing in now that he was gone and she wondered what he would think of her if she'd had the courage to ask him to stay. For long moments, she pondered the idea until the soft whir of an engine pulled her out of her daze.

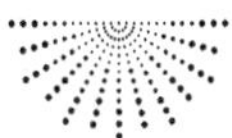

CHAPTER THIRTEEN

"Oooh! How could they say they don't believe in magic? Don't they know every time they denounce the existence of magic a cute little blond-haired, spoiled rotten fairy dies somewhere?" Mortianna complained, hoping Serephina wouldn't noticed the forced sincerity in her tone. Serephina's expression was rueful but Mortianna could see the strain their sister's absence caused, even if she only saw it around the otherwise well-tempered edges of her reactions. "It's a good thing we aren't fairies, right?"

Esmerelda's absence was driving them both insane but talking about their trouble didn't seem to help, which was why she had pulled out the scrying dish to peek in on Sam and Emma in the first place.

"Yes! Yes, it is." Turning to peer into the dish once more, Mortianna said, "What is wrong with people these days? Why is it so hard to admit there is something *more* at work in their lives when they feel the things love makes them feel?"

"Something great and grand and wonderful, right?" Serephina's wistful sigh slipped out on a broken breath. She glanced back into the scrying dish and waved her hand in the general direction of the couple they were watching. "We can't let this end badly, Morty."

"Nope!" Mortianna agreed in a cheery tone, crossing her legs beneath her. "Well, we could, but we aren't going to."

One at a time, she flipped up cards from the tarot deck. "No way we are going to sit back and do nothing. We aren't even going to placidly await the big decision from on high."

She turned over another card and smiled. "The CHG may have Esmerelda in their custody right now, thanks to the mix up with the quilt, but Sam and Emma's romance will show them we haven't lost our touch and we will get her back."

At least she hoped that was what would happen, but she didn't dare voice her own uncertainty out loud. Serephina was nutsy enough as it was and Merry had only been gone a few days. She started to flip up a third card, and hesitated, glancing instead at the scrying dish as if her gaze had been drawn there by something outside her control.

Her eyes widened. Dropping the deck, she clapped her hands together in glee. "Look, Feeny, she agreed! See?

What did I tell you? Esmerelda will be with us again in no time."

Beside her, Serephina shook a bottle Mortianna hadn't seen her retrieve. Vaguely, she might have recalled her sister mixing two parts red and one part green, but she wasn't sure until Serephina said, "Of course she is, Morty. This time, we can't fail. The potion ought to insure our success, but if not, the spell—"

There was an unusual quality to her sister's voice, too, one that spoke of determination regardless of consequence and it was one Mortianna could only ever recall this particular sister using once, a long, long time ago—and it had cost them twenty seven years of their life. On her feet in a flash, Mortianna snatched at the bottle. "Wait, don't do that!"

Serephina tried to keep the vial from her, blocking it with her body even as she held it out of Mortianna's immediate reach. "What? It's just a little cuddle spell. When Emma goes to dinner with Sam, she won't be able to resist curling up into his arms the minute he crooks his little finger."

But Mortianna was shaking her head while moving slowly closer to her sister. "Interference is not allowed, Feeny. How many times have you preached as much to me? I can't let you do it. Not when we aren't sure where Merry is or what is happening to her."

"You patently ignored every one of those sermons, Morty. Every single time I warned against the consequences, you just had to go ahead and wiggle those dainty fingers of yours and utterly break the rules. Well, look what happened!"

Mortianna moved closer, forcing her expression into one she hoped at least resembled contrition. "I apologized, Feeny. Every time. Besides, a nudge here, a swirl there to bring a couple close enough to touch? Insignificant. Admit it, Feeny. You know those tiny little bits of interference—if you can even call them that—were nothing compared to what you were about to do."

Serephina shook her head and a tear spilled onto her cheek. "Doesn't matter, Mortianna Seville. You still dabbled where you ought not and now our sweet Merry is gone."

Mortianna's eyes widened. "So you're blaming this on me? You're saying Merry's summons before the CHG is my fault? Hey, I'm not the one who was in such a blistering hurry to sneak out and read the Cupid Pact I forgot to do my job!"

Seeing her chance, Mortianna jumped. Serephina stumbled backward a couple steps—just enough to put the vial filled with the foul, purplish black liquid out of harms way. Serephina lost her grip on the bottle and it tumbled end over end, almost in slow motion, droplets flying until it came to rest on the thick carpet beneath the coffee table holding the scrying dish.

Flashing a look at her sister, Mortianna turned and picked up the bottle. "If you have to blame someone for Esmerelda's absence, maybe you'd better think back to the last time you dropped a bit of this into the scrying dish. Or better yet, just take a look in the mirror, Serephina."

~

SAM'S KITCHEN was filled with the scents of his efforts. Making dinner for a woman he actually wanted to spend time with was kind of a big deal to him, which was why he'd called in reinforcements: Jordan.

Only now, while he waited for his friend to give a thumbs up or down about the stew he had put together, he wondered if it was a good idea for Jordan to have information about the progress of his relationship with Emma Riley.

Not that Jordan wasn't hopeful and cheering him on every step of the way, in the way that guys do, which meant unmercifully ribbing him every chance he got. Both Jordan and Kaylee were supportive of his pursuit. But Jordan had a way of reminding Sam to keep things real that Sam wasn't particularly enthusiastic about this time around.

A clank of a spoon warned Sam that Jordan was taste-testing again without giving an opinion and he scowled. Jordan only grinned. Finally, he relented.

"Grandma Ellie would be proud, Samster. You whip this up from memory?" Jordan asked while filching another spoonful of broth from the pot beside him.

"Recipe, actually. The only thing I could remember was the smell. Once the kitchen took on a certain aroma,

I knew I had it right. Do you think Emma will like it?" Sam barely glanced in his direction before he snapped and hurried to the fridge.

"Can't have broth without bread for sopping." He pulled a loaf from the freezer with one hand and waved at Jordan with the other. "Get off the counter, by the way. We aren't nine anymore, you know."

"So Emma fixed *steak au poivre* for your dinner with her and you're making Country Bumpkin stew. You don't think she'll think you're cooking down on her, do you?" Jordan needled playfully and Sam snorted.

"Emma isn't pretentious, Jordan. Unlike some of my friends."

"Hey, I resemble that remark!" Jordan's pretended offense sounded clearly before he reminded Sam, "I'm not pretentious. I'm *spoiled*, thanks to my previous lucrative career, and there is a difference which I'd thank you to remember."

Sam gave him another snort. "Kaylee's rubbing off on you, I see."

Jordan's brow rose. "Kaylee rubbing?" he asked as he hopped off the counter. "Hmm, now that you mention it—"

Sam's hand flew up. "No, no no. I don't want to know."

Jordan's laughter pealed through the kitchen. "Oh, come on. You've been with Miss Riley what? Three times? And you still haven't made it to second base? Yeah,

I think you wanna know, Sam. You *really* wanna know. Especially the bit about—"

The back door slammed and Kaylee's voice filtered into the kitchen. "Don't you dare, Jordan Parker. Sam doesn't need to know the details of how you tried to steal second and ended up sliding into third at the ball park yesterday."

In the kitchen, she put the bags she was carrying on the table and went to Jordan where she lifted a cheek for his kiss, then said, "Michael isn't a very good referee. Neither is Jo for that matter. Besides, it was just luck that you got around me and you know it."

"So you were *lucky* to get to third base?" Sam's pointed question was followed by the spill of guffaws every bit as full and cheerful as Jordan's had been until that one's suddenly much less enthusiastic expression forced him to mute his amusement to a simple grin. "Now *that* was useful information. Thanks, Kaylee."

"Of course. Any time," she said, smiling up at him. Then, "Wait. I suddenly get the feeling you two weren't talking about baseball at all, were you?"

"Not exactly," Jordan admitted. "Why don't you explain what we were discussing, Sammy? Maybe Kaylee can give us both a few pointers."

Mock scowling at his friend, Sam shook his head. "Nevermind. You wouldn't want to know the depths of your fiance's depravity anyway, Kaylee. Not this close to the wedding."

Her nod of acceptance signaling a close to their

previous teasing, Sam went about readying the bread for the oven while Kaylee checked the stew.

"Wow, this is delicious, Sam. Emma is going to be pleasantly surprised. Mmm," she said, spooning another bite into her mouth. "A man who can cook like this is a man worth hanging on to."

"Is that a jab at my lack of skill?" Jordan pretended to pout until Kaylee reassured him his skills in the kitchen were nothing to be embarrassed about either and Sam bit his tongue to keep from going back to the slightly naughty round of conversation him and Jordan been about to have before.

"I'm hanging on to you," Kaylee reminded him. "Or had you forgotten whose ring I am currently wearing?"

Wiggling her fingers, she flashed said ring and Sam thought of the wedding band his grandmother had left him. Surprisingly enough, he also thought of Emma wearing it, and that had him hitting the breaks hard. No. The two of them had barely managed to get through one dinner together. It was way too soon to be having those sort of thoughts. But he couldn't seem to get them out of his head now that they were there.

"Hello? Earth to Sammy? Are you in there, sir?" Kaylee asked, snapping her fingers in front of Sam's face. A quick mental shake brought him round.

"Sorry, something popped into my head and I got lost in there. What did you need?"

"Jordan and I were asking if you'd asked Emma to join you at the wedding," she explained. "Have you?"

Emma. Joining him for a wedding. Well... He cleared his throat and reached for a towel to wipe his suddenly clammy palms. "Ah, no, I haven't. I wasn't aware I needed to bring a date?"

"Silly. You know we aren't requiring a plus one but if you want to bring Emma along, I was just letting you know we'd be happy to have her there." She gave Jordan a nudge. "Wouldn't we?"

"As if Sam would show up anywhere without a date if I have one," Jordan said. "Of course we would love it if Emma comes to the wedding with you, old man. Want me to ask her for you?"

Sam pretended to go for Jordan's throat after that crack and Jordan pretended to care. From the corner of his eye, Sam caught Kaylee rolling her eyes, but there was a hint of a smile curling her lips as well so he knew she didn't think their mock tussle was serious.

"Better take him in hand now, Kaylee, if you want anything left for the wedding night. Otherwise, I'm about to take him down," Sam warned.

Kaylee just laughed. "Be gentle, Sam. Last time you took him down for needling you, I had to coddle him for days."

"Yeah," Sam grunted in response to Jordan's fist playfully grinding his ribs. "He always was a mama's boy!"

"Hey, you leave Mama out of this. If you hadn't started it ..." Jordan complained and Sam found himself caught in a headlock.

A timid knock at the door brought all their heads swinging round. "Ah, hello? Is Sam here?"

Sam saw Kaylee motioning toward where he now lay sprawled in the floor between his kitchen and dining room, his head stuck in the crook of Jordan's arm, and she was grinning. "That's him. Don't worry, I'm about to take mine home now, so there won't be anymore rough-housing tonight. Well, unless you and Sam …"

"Emma! You're early," Sam interrupted, dislodging himself from Jordan's grasp so he could climb to his feet and greet her properly.

"Mm hmm, a little," she nodded. "But without the two grand a bottle champagne. Hope that's okay?" She glanced from him to Kaylee, to Jordan, and back again. "If you'd rather do this another day, Sam, I have things I could be doing—"

"Oh, no. We are doing this." Springing to his feet, Sam caught her by the elbow. "Emma Riley, this is Jordan Parker and his fiancee, Kaylee Dean."

Turning to his friends, he said, "Jordan, Kaylee, you remember the book I was telling you about? Well, this is Emma, the author. She's having dinner with me tonight. You two are not."

Kaylee laughed. "See, Jordan? You were worried for nothing. Sam's perfectly comfortable being himself with his new girlfriend."

Sam watched Emma's face color even as she stuttered out a hasty but useless correction. "He's not, I mean I'm not—"

He pulled her forward to his side so the two of them were looking at Jordan and Kaylee and cast his friends a mock scowl. "Don't bother. These two are beyond correction."

Then he smiled. "Jordan and Kaylee are getting married in a few months and they'd like you to come to the wedding. With me. Any chance you'd put on a spiffy dress and walk beside me for a few hours in a month or two?"

"Oh, there's no need to rush her for an answer, Sam," Kaylee hurried to explain. "But it's true. We would love to have you there. Think about it? Meantime, we need to go, Jordan. Sam has this lovely dinner prepared and I need to stop by the shelter. It was a pleasure to finally meet you, Miss Riley."

"Looking forward to your book debut launch party thing at the re-opening of the One Shot, too." Jordan offered with a nod. His hand at the small of Kaylee's back, Jordan led her out the back door, calling over his shoulder as he went. "See ya later, Sam. Don't do anything I wouldn't!"

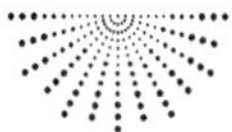

CHAPTER FOURTEEN

Sam's somewhat sheepish smile did nothing to quell the anxiety already rising inside her as Jordan and Kaylee left, nor did the quiet comforts of his surprisingly cozy kitchen. Her gaze flitted from the warm oak cabinetry to the deep double-bowl ceramic sink to the cool white and blue checked floor, somehow registering how much the room practically echoed with sentiment for good times, great friends, and delicious home-cooked meals while she impatiently waited for Sam to say goodbye to his friends.

Sam closed the door behind them and had barely managed to turn back to her before she began to protest. To refuse, actually, in no uncertain terms, anything to do with a large public gathering she was expected to attend. "No. No launch party. I won't. How could you do this, Sam?"

She didn't give him time to answer. Depositing the

bag she had brought in with her on the fluffy blue and white checkered and padded seat cushion of one of the chairs at his breakfast bar, she turned to face him while her fingers tugged at the hem of her burgundy sweater, straightening it beneath her coat, and shook her head. "You can have the quilt and the puzzle. Both are in the bag. Sorry about dinner, but I'm leaving now."

Turning on her heel, she marched toward the door, but Sam's arm shot out, stopping her.

"Why are you always leaving me? Don't you know I have issues with that, woman? Look, you don't have to do a thing, Emma. Not with the book, not at the One Shot, but you *did* agree to have dinner with me tonight and the one has nothing to do with the other. Think about that before you walk out of here without tasting my grand-mother's stew recipe."

"I could care less about the stew!" Her arms flew upward gesticulating her exasperation. "I don't know if you've noticed or not, but I'm not like you, Sam! I'm not —I'm not a people person. I'm *shy*, and quiet, and non-assuming."

His brows rose. "You mean as opposed to the raging female I see before me now?"

Emma rolled her eyes, closed them, and groaned. Somehow, she kept forgetting *this* Sam wasn't the man she knew intimately from her dreams and could freely express herself to. *This* Sam was practically a stranger. Still, she had to make sure he knew she wasn't about to start dancing to his tune whenever he thought to play

Emma Radio. "This doesn't count. This is—I don't know what this is or why I'm even bothering to discuss this with you *at all*, but you have to know I am not going to be at any party for the launch of a book I never intended to publish in the first place—a party you've obviously already set up on my behalf without asking me. Again!"

"On *my* behalf," Sam quietly corrected. Now that she wasn't actively headed for the door, he'd relaxed his stance a bit. He even looked a little uninterested now with his hands resting lightly on the back of one of the three other chairs nestled up to the breakfast bar. What had he said about issues? The question niggled at the edge of her thoughts but he was still talking so she ignored it for the moment.

"The book launch was planned by *me* to benefit *my* business. It's a book about coffee that I think my customers will enjoy, remember? If it helps you sell books that is good, too. You don't have to show up if you prefer not to, but I would be infinitely happier if you did."

His last words were like a bucket of ice water flowing over her. Her presence wasn't necessary but would be appreciated? Was that what he was saying? What he'd intended all along? Great. She had over-reacted. Again. Lowering her chin, she pinned her gaze to the floor about eight inches from his feet. "I'm sorry for my outburst. It was apparently uncalled for."

"Do you do that a lot?" At her questioning look, elaborated. "Do you freak out over the thought of appearing in public? Over the possibility of being recognized or noticed in a crowd?"

Did she? Emma cocked her head to the side, considering. Before college, she would have given an immediate 'no,' but now? "Maybe."

"Except with me, of course. You never seem to have any confidence issues or hangups when it's just you and me." His lopsided grin had an immediate effect, warming and relaxing her, and she smiled back, but her mind was spinning over the revelation he'd just given her.

Was she different with him? "Only because you bring out the worst in me."

"How is that, I wonder?" Sam countered. "Such willingness to be open and forthright usually stems from trust built over a period of time or an indescribable but instant affinity with someone, but you and I..."

Emma waited with baited breath for him to finish, which he did after he'd retrieved a pair of bowls and dished both full from the steaming pot on the stove and carried them to the table. Motioning with a quick tilt of his head which she assumed was a signal that she should follow him, he led her through the kitchen into the windowed dining nook where he deposited the bowls— heavy earthenware soup crocks actually, then turned back to take her coat, hanging it on a peg by the back door before he went to the kitchen again for silverware, and then joined her at the table.

"You and I, we've only been in each others company a handful of times and for most of those other people were present—people whom, if I correctly recall, you either ignored or were passingly polite to, when and if the matter warranted," he pointed out. "But you've never been particularly hesitant or shy about speaking your mind to me. What gives?"

Comfort.

Emma almost blurted out the word but held it back while she examined what it meant for her to feel comfortable with Sam Huntingdon, III. From the moment she'd first seen him in Sevilles, he had caused reactions in her, mostly because he was so blasted good-looking she'd had a hard time looking away from him. Covert study from beneath one's lashes counted as legitimate research, right? Only Sam was not her subject and she had not been writing a discourse on attraction or a lack thereof. And then there were the dreams which had been so vivid, so consuming, it had led to a feeling of intimate connection whenever she ended up in his presence in real life …

"While we wait for you to mull it over, why not have a bite of the stew?" Sam suggested, his words breaking into her thoughts, and Emma did not miss either the humor or the tiniest edge of sarcasm in his tone. Nor had she neglected to realize how deftly he had led her to his table for dinner although she had fully intended to leave but a moment ago.

Seating himself across from her, he unfolded a napkin in his lap and took up his spoon, waving it over his bowl as he explained, "My Grandma Ellie used to make this exact stew every Sunday evening during the winter. She knew Dad would be dropping me off before heading out on another week-long cross-country haul and her stew, she said, would stick to our ribs and keep us plenty warm until Dad came home again."

"Memories," Emma murmured before settling herself to scoop up a bite of the stew. Like the ones of her older brothers, she admitted, which had flitted through her thoughts earlier when she'd come inside to find Sam and his friend rough-housing on the kitchen floor. The ones that had incited the tiniest feeling of homesickness in her —something she hadn't felt in quite some time. "Your grandmother was helping you create good memories of your dad."

Between bites, Sam considered what she'd said for a moment, then nodded. "I think you're right. Grandma Ellie always did have a way of connecting things that comforted me the most with Dad."

"Hmm," she murmured, reaching for the glass Sam had already filled with sweet iced tea from the pitcher on the table. "Like quilts?"

"No," Sam said, his voice much quieter now. "The quilts remind me of my mother."

His expression changed and Emma had a sinking feeling she'd touched on a subject Sam wasn't at all comfortable with. "Your mother?"

Sam nodded. "She passed away when I was too young to remember a whole lot about her but old enough to miss her for the rest of my days, if that makes sense. For years, it was just me and my dad but his schedule didn't allow much home time. Grandpa and Grandma Ellie did their best to create a stable life for me but for the longest, I lived for the weekends when Dad would be home so he could tell me stories about Mama."

Emma's smile was hesitant. She wasn't sure she wanted to hear the story of the quilt, if there was one. She was already feeling too much empathy for this man with sandy hair and beautiful eyes. She already wanted to put her arms around him, too, but for entirely different reasons. If she allowed sympathy and desire to collide in her mind, there might be trouble—more than she could handle. Still, she laid her spoon beside her bowl and crossed her hands in her lap. "One of the stories your father told about your mom had something to do with a quilt, I suppose. Want to share?"

Sam shook his head. "Actually, there was no such story. I'm not sure why quilts tend to make me think of Mama, to be honest, but I think it probably has something to do with feeling secure—a feeling Grandma Ellie continued to instill by wrapping me in the softest ones she owned every time Dad brought me inside."

"The one you bought out from under me," he continued with a teasing arch of a brow, "was a bit of sentimental reminder. The black and white simplicity of it made me think of opposites."

His lips twisted into a wry smile. "And attraction."

He shrugged. "Then and now, mother and son, life and death. Man. Woman. Each so utterly different and yet connected in a way that says no matter the differences, regardless of the juxtapositions of life, we are still and will always be bound. We are together. Never apart, or alone, or even cold and lonely."

He took a deep breath and Emma covertly raised a hand to hastily wipe away a tear. Taking up her spoon, she chanced a look at his face and found him watching her intently.

"Opposites do not attract arbitrarily, Emma. They are immutably bonded at the level of the soul."

Oh, wow. If he kept talking like that ...

Taking a deep breath herself, she blew at a curl which had fallen in front of her face and smiled before taking up her spoon again to taste the stew his grandma had made for him when she was alive; the simple meal he was obviously proud to have made. And he'd made it for her. She wondered if she should feel honored? "Well, ah, hmm. You were right. The stew is delicious, Sam. Your grandmother would be proud."

His low chuckle threaded its way along her spine, making her want to squirm in her chair. "Conversation's a little too deep for you, huh?"

"Personal," Emma corrected. So much so, she was having trouble meeting his gaze now. "A little too personal."

"Right. Personal." Sam nodded and resettled himself in his chair. "So let's talk about something else. Something I've been real curious about lately."

Relieved that he wasn't upset over her need to move

the conversation into a more neutral territory, Emma nodded and let her gaze roam over his features, noting the way his shirt clung to his broad shoulders and hugged his chest while she waited for him to tell her what had caught his attention. "Curiosity could be good. As a matter of fact, you put me in mind of a cat in that you seem the type whose curiosity might never be appeased. But go ahead, tell me. What have you been curious about?"

Lifting her gaze, his laughter-warmed eyes locked with hers and darkened, as if he had read and correctly interpreted the sudden change in the direction of her thoughts. Emma felt the heat of his stare all the way to her toes. In fact, she thought she might well drown in the pooling desire she saw now in his eyes.

She thought she would be more than happy to give up breathing so long as he kept looking at her like that—until he leaned forward and caught one of her hands in his, causing heat to spiral through her and a tingling sensation to begin somewhere deep in her core.

"*You.* I'm curious about you, Emma Riley," he said. "Who are you? What makes you tick? Why do you consider yourself shy and unassuming? What turned you off being around people? Why do you keep quiet when I can see an entire universe of eager thoughts spinning in your eyes?"

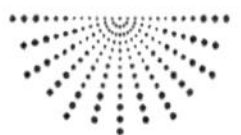

CHAPTER FIFTEEN

Watching her closely, Sam held his breath and waited, sure Emma would get up and walk out on him now that he'd turned the conversation to her. But what he'd said was true. He genuinely wanted to know more about her—a lot more—although he hadn't a clue why his simple curiosity felt like a whole lot more.

Her answers, whatever they may be, were important to him. He realized he needed to know what drove her, what made her who she was—and right now, who she was was the woman he felt more in tune with, more attracted to than any other he'd thought he wanted over the past six years.

Obviously, she had people issues, but who didn't have issues of one kind or another these days? He himself still found it hard to deal with being left behind when someone he cared about went away for extended periods of time. Probably due to his mother's untimely death and his father's job, sure, but those problems were still there. They hadn't disappeared just because he realized where they came from.

"I'm no puzzle, Sam. Nor a riddle to be solved." She shrugged. "I'm just a girl who had her illusions shattered early on about what people do and do not find interesting.

"Intelligence and a thirst for knowledge doesn't matter much when it's housed inside an awkward girl with springy red hair and freckles who asks a million questions a mile a minute and eventually becomes a nuisance to everyone who knows her."

Sam sensed a deep pain behind those words—the pain of what must have been a thousand rejections over a lifetime in response to her intense curiosity—and he knew. He understood why she had become a research specialist rather than an entrepreneur. He knew why she tended to shun people and hide behind her glasses and her job. He knew without asking what had made her retreat into herself rather than stand out, stand up, and show the world what she was made of.

"You didn't want to compete, did you? Friends. Family," he explained. "You didn't want to compete for their attention, or even their affection. Now, when someone comes along who sees what you've been hiding all these years, you don't trust their interest and enthusiasm because it's given freely and you don't understand how or why."

Tilting her head to the side, Emma pushed her now empty bowl aside and lay down her spoon before casting him a semi-teasing glare. "Can we please stop analyzing me now, Dr. Sam?"

He laughed. "Only if you promise to stop trying to hide. You don't have to do that, Emma. Not with me. I can see you—the *real* you—and I like what I see. I'm just waiting for you realize you are safe with me and that there's no need to compete for anything you might want that I have to offer. It's already yours."

A nervous laugh jittered from her lips. "You do realize you're getting awfully close to uttering one of those cheesy movie lines, right?"

Grinning, Sam said, "You mean the ones all women secretly long to hear? The ones that leave them sighing dreamily and crying happy tears? I didn't know."

This time her laugh was full and warm. "You're such a ham, Sam Huntingdon. No wonder everyone loves you."

"Even you?" He didn't stop to think about what she might read into his question. He just blurted it out and went on although he did notice the subtle change in her gaze, the slight flush on her cheeks, and the way she carefully avoided looking at him. "Well, if I had known winning you over was going to be *that* easy, I wouldn't have bothered with the stew. I'd have gone straight to the introductions."

"Introductions?"

Sam nodded. "Yes. I believe it's customary for a man to introduce his lady to the ruler of the house."

Turning in his chair, he pushed it away from the table, snapped his fingers and called out, "Jabez! Come here, boy. Come here. Come inside and meet Emma."

A scuffling noise was soon followed by the sound of toenails clicking on the floor, and then a black and white blur with bright blue eyes rushed at Sam, not stopping until his front paws were in Sam's lap and his moist nose inches from his master's. *"Arff! Arff!"*

Sam pulled back slightly but immediately reached out to ruffle the dog's fur. "Whew. Doggie breath. Haven't had your doggie biscuit today, have you?"

"Arff!" the Husky pup replied and Sam chuckled. "Emma, this is Jabez. One of the Huskies at the shelter was abandoned before she dropped her litter. When they came, Kaylee asked me if I would like to adopt one. I took one look at this handsome fellow and could not resist."

"I can see why. He's a cutey. Hello, Jabez. Hello," Emma crooned to the pup. Jabez turned his head and looked at her but he didn't leave Sam for an instant. Sam playfully admonished him for neglecting to show "his lady" some love but Emma said it was perfectly fine. "At least he isn't screeching and trying to claw my eyes out like Chloe did to you."

"No worries. Chloe was just protecting her mistress from potential threats, as she should."

"So you admit to being a potential threat?"

"Absolutely. To your boredom. Loneliness. And any chance of your spending the rest of what's left of these cold winter nights alone." He wiggled his brows up and down and Emma laughed. "Beware, Emma. My boyish good looks and charming good nature makes slipping into your daily routine, and thereafter your life, a matter of ease. One minute I'm on the fringes, and the next?"

He snapped his fingers. "I'm up close and very personally real in every aspect of your life."

"It's a good thing I haven't let down my guard, then. Otherwise you'd be stealing into my business, my quiet, peaceful dinnertime, *and* my dreams. Oh, wait..." She gave him a side-wise look, then rolled her eyes, but she was smiling.

"Ah, yes, those *dreams*. You never did tell me what they were about."

"Nor am I going to." Sliding her chair back, Emma stood and calling for the puppy, she snapped her fingers like he had. Jabez, always ready for affection, defected immediately. He rushed over, jumping up to rest his feet on Emma's waist.

"Goodness, you're a strong one! There's a good boy," she said. Steadying herself in the face of his enthusiasm, she scrubbed her fingers playfully through his fur. "I'll bet you would make Chloe behave herself, even on her most inventive days, hmm? Do you like cats, Jabez?"

"For breakfast," Sam said, then, at her look of abject horror, he laughed. "I'm teasing. He's never met an animal he didn't like—yet. You should bring Chloe with you next time and we'll see how the two of them get along."

Squatting in the floor, Emma snapped her fingers in the air, encouraging Jabez to jump up and down beside her. Each time he did, she'd give him a scratch, which he loved. "Why would there be a next time?"

"Because you like me? And because I'm asking nicely?" Getting to his feet, Sam snapped his fingers and said, "Out, Jabez. We'll be along in a minute."

The Husky pup obviously knew what 'out' meant because he dropped immediately to the floor and ran to the doggy door on the back door off the kitchen.

To Emma, he said, "Will you come back tomorrow? We'll have lunch this time and I'll show you the workshop out back. There's no lathe, but you can see the *chiffonier* Jordan's restoring for me for the One Shot."

"No lathe, huh? I don't know," she teased. "There should really be a lathe."

Stuffing his hands in his pockets, Sam twisted side to side in a rocking motion the way a nervous teen might and said, "I'll buy one in the morning if you'll say yes."

Emma laughed. "A girl could get to like you really fast, Mr. Huntingdon. You're so accommodating."

He shook his head, denying her statement. "I just know what I want, Miss Riley, and what I want is you."

EMMA FELT her reaction to his declaration all the way to her toes. The truth was she wanted him, too. But she wasn't sure he would be able to handle what having her would mean. Not Sam. He was a people person. A charmer. He loved to go places and see things and talk to people wherever he went. Being with her would curtail a lot of that.

Not to mention her preoccupation with needing fidelity right from the start. If Sam wanted to be with her, he would have to be with her only—even if they were only going out a few nights a week. If she couldn't hold his interest for a week or two without him supplementing his lifestyle with other women, there was no hope whatsoever for a lifetime of monogamy.

Maybe that would be the perfect test, a way for her to find out how serious he really was about wanting her, about being curious and hoping to get to know her better. Or, she could have misread him altogether. Maybe he'd meant he wanted her, like, right now—as in a one-night fling thing?

"What are you thinking?"

"I'm wondering what you meant when you said you want me." Peering at him from beneath lowered lashes, she asked, "Care to explain?"

His brows lowered. "How many ways can one take 'I want you'? I meant exactly what I said."

Emma shook her head. "No, no, no. There are a lot of ways what you said could be construed, and you know it. Are you looking for friendship? An over-nighter? A short fling? A long-term affair? Or maybe you're hoping for the real relationship Macoy?"

Meeting his questioning gaze full on, she said, "Before I agree to see you again, I need to know, Sam."

"Because you're an all or nothing kind of girl?" he half-teased, but she could tell he was partially serious. And the part of him that wasn't? The side that still insisted on being playful? She wasn't in the mood for it right now.

"No, because I don't want to be hurt and the easiest way to avoid that is to know what I'm getting myself into from the get-go." Blunt might be revealing and a bit hard-edged, but in her experience, it kept one from being confused or having doubts later.

His stare said more eloquently than his lips how odd he found her to be. "You're a tough nut to crack, Emma Riley, you know that?"

"I am what I am, Sam. Oddities, eccentricities, call my determination and need to know the truth up front whatever you like but they aren't going to go away and they aren't going to change." At least she hoped they didn't. Bending the rules for Sam, no matter how much she might wish she could, would be a Very Bad Thing.

"Fair enough. Alright, let's see … I assume you also require total honesty, right?"

His tone was light, but Emma knew by the look in his eyes that he was finally being as serious as she was. "Right—which means you'd probably better think about all this before you answer. Maybe you'll decide you don't want me as badly as you think you do."

"Oh, there's no chance of that, Emma," he promised,

his voice husky. "I am absolutely, one hundred percent certain I want you. I'm just trying to figure out how to explain how much to you without scaring you away."

Holding up one hand, Emma put a smidge of space between her index finger and her thumb. "This much?"

Sam shook his head. "More than that."

She held both hands about six inches apart. "This much?"

Again, he shook his head no, so she widened the gap. But before she could ask again if it were enough, he reached out and pulled her against his chest. Emma blinked in surprise, her gaze flying up to meet his.

"*This* much, Emma, and a whole lot more," he said in the seconds before his mouth crushed down on hers in a kiss far too long denied.

CHAPTER SIXTEEN

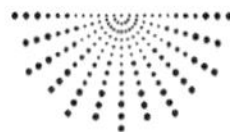

*E*mma leaned into his kiss, letting go, for the moment, of her insecurities about where they might be headed. His mouth was warm on hers, his kiss seeking. Insistent and yet gentle. Dimly, Emma realized this was the first time he'd kissed her that she hadn't immediately thought she'd slipped back into her dreams. The man kissing her now was the real Sam, and the knowledge was electrifying.

No, wait. It wasn't knowledge creating a vibration in her gut, she realized—it was a cell phone. Breaking away from the kiss, she said, "Maybe you should get that. It might be important."

Sam groaned in disappointment, but stepped back to remove the phone from the clip on his belt. "Sam here. Elliot, hi. What's up?"

While Sam spoke with whomever had called, Emma wandered around the kitchen that looked more like it should belong to Martha Stewart or maybe even Sara Lee than Sam Huntingdon, III. It wasn't utilitarian at all. Rather, it seemed homey and well used. Casting a wondering glance over her shoulder at Sam, she marveled over the man who apparently had such a passion for cooking. Her father never cooked. Neither had either of her brothers.

"Grandma," Sam mouthed, having caught her questioning gaze. Ending the call, he slipped the phone back onto the clip and leaned against a counter, crossing his arms over his chest. "Grandma's kitchen was *the* central focus of my life for so many years, it kind of makes sense that I would carry the security of it over into adulthood."

"Now there's a security blanket you can't tote around with you," Emma teased.

"Right. But there's somewhere I want to carry *you*— my office, unless you'd rather walk?" He grinned, then pointed to his cell phone and explained. "That was Elliot Drummond, the architectural engineer who is overseeing the renovations at the cafe. He called to let me know he was faxing over some blueprints I thought you might want to see."

Curious, Emma asked, "Me? Blueprints for?"

"Coffee Cozy. Latte Lounge. Espresso Escape. The comfy, informal little drink-coffee-and-lounge-around-in-semi-privacy buildings you sketched for me, remember? Elliot used your drawings and a ton of measurements that took him practically all day to get and put together... " He'd straightened from his lounging position against the counter and was headed toward a hallway when he realized he was alone and turned back. Holding out a hand to her, he asked, "You coming or not?"

Emma debated whether or not she should follow him into the obviously more private, personal areas of his house. Maybe she should decline and wait for him here? Sam didn't seem to care either way. In fact, he seemed perfectly unconcerned. Was his unconcern because the person he'd invited back was her? Or did he bring anyone and everyone into his home office for a look at blueprints when they were over?

She thought of his friends, Kaylee and Jordan. Sam would invite them back without a thought. But they were his *friends*. She was just an acquaintance. Wasn't she? "I—yes, I would love to see the blueprints."

Sam nodded, his hand falling to rest at the small of her back when she joined him. As he lead her through the short hallway and across his living room to his office, he finished what he'd been saying. "Elliot put together a set of workable blueprints for each, but he also sent over —I don't know what you call them, but it's a set of images showing where each of the buildings could be placed. Structural arrangement or something like that?"

Waving away the matter as unimportant, he disappeared into the room and came back a few seconds later with a stack of papers the size of poster board. He pointed toward the sofa. "We'll sit over there and you can tell me what you think."

And that was when Emma became lost.

Lost in the moment, in the excitement of seeing her idea for a project coming closer to life, in the easy back and forth chatter between her and Sam—the kind of to and fro discussion that felt as natural to her as breathing —over Elliot's proposed locations, dimensions, interior decoration, even how the wait-staff would handle the little tea-room like structures he was seriously considering having put in where she'd drawn them on the back lot.

"I like you like this," Sam said later, during a lull in the conversation. "All passionately animated and genuinely interested enough in this project to forget all about being shy or inhibited. You've been like a kid at Christmas from the moment we sat down together in here."

Emma turned her head, glancing up at him in confusion, and almost bumped noses with him. There was a mischievous glint in his eyes. She flushed. How had she not noticed how close they were? He was right there beside her on the sofa, his thigh touching hers. She even vaguely recalled letting her palm rest on it once or twice, now that she thought about it, but he'd said nothing.

He must have been enjoying her distraction because he had one arm around her, too, from where he'd leaned over to point something out on the blueprint earlier and needed to brace himself, but then left it there—for the fun of it?

How cozy the two of them had become during the past fifteen or so minutes, Emma thought. Uncomfortable now, she pulled away from Sam, pushed her glasses up on her nose with one hand and then ran both palms along her thighs.

"Don't," Sam directed, reaching out to catch one of her hands in his. "There's no need to get all stuffy just because you've suddenly realized we were getting along fine together."

"It scares me," she said, accidentally blurting out the truth. Cutting a quick look in his direction, she got up and headed back into the kitchen. It was clearly time for her to leave.

Glancing at her watch, she gasped. *Eleven thirty?* Where in the world had the time gone?

"Thank you for dinner. The stew was delicious," she called over her shoulder while sliding her arms into her coat. "If your grandmother were alive, she would be proud of you, I'm sure."

"Grandma Ellie was proud of me before I made stew," Sam said from behind her, his warm breath fanning the tiny hairs at her nape, sending tingles along her spine while his hands joined hers as he helped her with her coat. He tugged her around for a brief yet somehow lingering kiss. "Thank you for coming tonight, Emma. I've really enjoyed these past few hours with you."

Reaching into her pocket, Emma made sure she hadn't forgotten to put her keys in there. She nodded. "I enjoyed tonight, as well."

Sam walked with her to the door, then leaned against the jamb and waited until she reached her car to ask the question he'd wanted to ask before she got all antsy in the living room and decided to leave. "Will you come by the One Shot tomorrow, Emma? We're officially closed for the next few weeks, but Elliot will be there to break ground on the cozies. You could mention those tweaks you pointed out to me a few minutes ago. See what he says..."

She opened the car door and slid inside. "Not this time. I have to work. Goodnight, Sam. Thanks again for a lovely evening."

Watching her leave, Sam felt the chill of the night close in around him but he waited until he could no longer see her taillights before he went inside, locking the door behind him. Silence settled in, enveloping him in a sense of loneliness that seemed heavier now that Emma was gone.

Shutting off the lights as he went through the kitchen where they'd shared Grandma Ellie's delightful stew to the living room where they'd spent more than an hour chatting about the renovations at the coffee cafe and her ideas that he'd decided to incorporate, Sam wondered why getting her involved had come to mean so much to him. All he could figure was that he hoped if she were invested in the cafe, in his business even if only in a small way, she would somehow become invested in him.

Was it wrong? He wondered. Maybe he shouldn't use the book and the construction of her ideas as bait to lure her to him. Maybe he should just lay everything out on the table with her and let Emma decide. Dropping onto the sofa, Sam stretched out his feet to one side and blew out a harsh sigh. If he weren't so afraid she would ignore him and walk away without giving the two of them a chance, he probably would.

Obviously, Emma Riley had a superpower where he was concerned. It seemed she alone had the power to eat away at his confidence until he was left yearning and yet too unsure of himself to let her know what he wanted. What he felt.

It scares me, she had said, and Sam wished he knew why. What had happened in her past to make getting close to someone a thing she feared? Who had hurt her so badly she'd come out of the episode skittish and closed and utterly relationship-shy?

~

"HER FATHER. Hello? It was her father, father, father! " Mortianna called to Sam in the scrying dish before glancing over her shoulder at Serephina. "Why are guys so blind when it comes to their ability to see this stuff?"

"Possibly because it wasn't her father?" Serephina pointed out. Hooking her purse over her shoulder, she held up a set of keys. "I'm going to the library."

"Nope!" Recognizing the set her sister held from a time when there were no such thing as revolving doors, or even sliding ones that did not operate on magic alone, Mortianna leaned back and leveraged up, scooting backward several inches to do so, given how close she'd been sitting to the coffee table, and bounced hastily to her feet. "No, no, no Feeny. You don't need to do that. Give me the keys."

The glare her sister gave her should have scorched her eyeballs from the sockets but luckily, Mortianna's eyeballs were fully anti-scorch at this point in her life. "Serephina, don't glare. It makes you look—mean."

"He knows where she is, Morty," Serephina declared. "Maybe the CHG did not take Esmerelda at all. Have you thought about that? What if Alastair has her locked away in one of those chambers off the catacombs down there?"

"Why would he? Come on, Feeny. You know what happened as well as I do. We botched yet another assignment and Merry got the pinch for it. The CHG—"

Serephina shook her head adamantly. "No. It's more than that, Morty. I've been having dreams. Nightmares, actually, ever since Merry disappeared and I think something is wrong—so wrong I no longer believe her disappearance has anything to do with the CHG."

"You didn't tell me you'd been having dreams. What were they?"

"Just silly dreams about Cupid being attacked by his own bow," Serephina shrugged. "But it's so terrifying, Mortianna, so *real*."

Flipping the keys into her palm, she turned toward the door. "I have to go."

"Wait!" Mortianna caught her by the shoulders, halting her. "You're dreaming about Cupid, bows, and attacks. You think they're a sign, that your dreams have something to do with Esmerelda's disappearance, but not the Cupid Heart Guard?"

Holding up both hands, she waved them about in front of Serephina's worried eyes. "Cupid? Bows? Hello?" Leading her sister away from the door and toward the sofa, Mortianna urged her to sit. Returning to her cross-legged seating position but this time on the couch instead of the floor, she continued. "Put the keys away, Feeny, and tell me what you dreamed. And don't leave out any details, no matter how silly you think they might be. One of them could be important."

"You're patronizing, aren't you?" Serephina accused, her eyes narrowing in suspicion, but Mortianna hurriedly assured her she was not.

"Absolutely not patronizing. I'm as worried about Esmerelda as you are but I don't want to rush out ill-prepared to storm the Keeper's gates with accusations of kidnapping without something a little more substantial to lean on."

"Alastair was the last person to see her, Mortianna. If we reported this to Michael Leavy, who do you think would be the first to end up in cuffs?"

"Alastair, probably," Mortianna admitted. "Or Airrick. Or both and I shudder to think where Hawthorne Grove would we be if both our Keepers were suddenly incarcerated. But we aren't sure Merry's been taken by anyone, remember? When we went to the library, Alastair said he'd seen her but then she disappeared. He didn't mention her being with anyone. He didn't say he'd seen her meet with anyone outside. What if she decided to do her research into the missing Cupid Pact thing some-where else?"

"Where, Morty? Another country? Even if she had, she would have known we would worry about her when she didn't come back. She would have found a way to get in touch, to let us know she is okay, but she hasn't. It has been days without a word from her. Not a single word. That isn't like Merry and you know it's not, Mortianna. She would have let us know."

Much as Mortianna hated to admit it, Serephina was right. It wasn't like Esmerelda to disappear for days on end without a word, and if the CHG didn't have her—which was Feeny's current worry—then someone or something surely did. Was Esmerelda in danger?

A chill chased its way down her spine, making her shiver, but she hid her reaction under a little wiggle as if she were merely trying to make herself more comfort-able on the sofa. "Dreams. Tell me about your night-mares, Feeny. If there's even a hint in them that says we should be worried about Esmerelda, I promise we will leave immediately for the library. I will personally help you interrogate Alastair and he will tell us everything he knows—even if we have to use a little dirty magic."

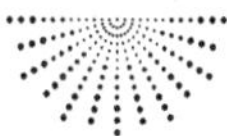

At nine thirty the following morning, Emma's phone rang. It was Sam.

"Are you sure you can't break away from whatever you're doing this morning? They're arguing and neither of them really have a clue what they are talking about."

Emma was still caught up in the research she was working on, her thoughts so deep into the thread she'd been following, she barely caught a word he'd said. "Huh? Who is arguing? Sam, it's not even ten o'clock yet and I'm working."

"So am I, Emma, or I'm trying to, but your friend won't leave Elliot alone and let him do his job."

Emma thought she heard a note of humor in his voice, and distracted as she was, she decided he was just having a go at her to try and get her to come to the One Shot although she had specifically told him last night she wouldn't be available today. "My friend? I don't have any friends in—oh, wait. Lindsay is there?"

Emma knew she was. She could hear her chattering in the background but it sounded like normal talk, not arguing.

"Yep, good old Lindsay. Something about a charm bracelet she lost on the lot over the weekend. You wouldn't know anything about that, would you?"

Putting a hand to her forehead, Emma dredged herself out of her research long enough to think. *Charm bracelet. Charm bracelet.* Snapping mental fingers, Emma tried to remember the last time she and Lindsay had talked, and whether or not a charm bracelet had been involved. Yes, she remembered now. She'd given it to Lindsay right after she'd picked up the quilt at Seville's. It had been attached to some loose threads in a fold of the coverlet. "Let me talk to her, please."

There was a moment of silence, then, "Hello? Who is this? Sam, why am I talking on your phone? Wait, Sam?"

"Lindsay? Hello, it's me, Emma. Lindsay, are you listening?" For whatever reason, Sam had called her to resolve some issue Lindsay was having with his architectural engineer when he shouldn't have gotten involved in the first place. If Lindsay had lost the bracelet, he should just let her look for it until she decided it was nowhere to be found. She would have given up eventually, but now...

"Emma? Oh my God, is that you? This is Sam's phone, I know it is, so... Sam has your number? Wow. And I thought there were no secrets between the two of us.

Were you going to tell me?" There was accusation in her tone, but Emma didn't have time to let her go there with the conversation. "I'm supposed to tell you you're holding up progress. To tell you to look for the bracelet wherever you last remember oooh-ing and aaah-ing over it. Yes, I'm telling you both of those. Now, I have to get back to work, so please, just find the bracelet and leave Mr. Drummond to whatever it is he is supposed to be doing."

Laughter. Warm, genuinely excited laughter filled her ear. "Emma, the bracelet isn't lost. I mean, it *was* lost, but Elliot found it. He gave it to me this morning, but there was an extra charm on it—one that wasn't there when you gifted the bracelet to me. Do you remember?"

Emma blew out an exasperated breath and rested her forehead on her palm. "How can I remember what I've never even seen? If the charm is new, I couldn't possibly—"

"No, not the new charm, silly. The old ones. The ones that were there before. Do you recall how many charms were on the bracelet initially?"

"Five," Emma blurted, knowing she'd never get off the phone otherwise. "There were five."

"Yes! A flower, a ladybug, a lace glove, a ladies hat, and a book. But this morning, when Elliot returned the bracelet to me, there were *six* charms. The new charm is a *lace fan*, Emma. A Victorian lace fan! Well, it's pewter, actually, but isn't that exquisite?"

"Utterly," Emma murmured. "Maybe a charm fairy

took the bracelet and added a new one for you as a surprise? Look, I really have to get back to work now, so tell..."

"You have to see it, Em," Lindsay declared without letting her finish, and Emma moved the phone away from her ear to stare at it in awe.

Had everyone at the One Shot lost their mind this morning? First, Sam wanted her to play referee between the engineer and interior designer he had hired, and now her best friend was insisting she simply must see a charm bracelet she had already seen. "Lindsay, I've seen it. I gave the thing to you, remember?"

"Oh, no, not the bracelet. The layout. Of these genius little coffee nook things Sam's having built at the back of the cafe. Whoever came up with the idea is pure brilliant!"

Sure Lindsay had meant to stroke Sam's ego with her praise, Emma still felt the heat of a blush slide over her cheeks because she knew who the genius was behind those designs, behind the entire idea. "Thank you."

"Wait, this is you? Sam Huntingdon, you've been holding out on me! Emma drew those sketches? *My* Emma?" The rustling of paper could be heard over the line, and then, "Of course you did. How did I not recognize it immediately. You have a certain style that few, if any, could imitate. And now I'm hurt. If you've spent enough time with Sammy here to come up with sketches for blueprints, there's definitely something going on between you two. You aren't getting married, are you?"

Emma's head almost smacked her computer screen she lifted it from her hand so fast. "Married? Sam and me? No. Oh, no. Lindsay, I *have* to go now. Put Sam back on, please?"

"Here ya go, she wants you," Emma heard Lindsay say, then Sam's low, huskily murmured "likewise" sent even more heat spiraling through her than the first sound of his voice had.

For a minute, dream and reality blended so well in her thoughts it felt almost as if she'd truly known this man for months now. Shared intimate conversations with him. Gone for long walks, watched hours worth of chick flicks on DVD with him while he held her, shared the same spoon for ice cream.

For an instant, she could almost believe she and Sam had shared far more intimate things than a kiss or two, but in reality … in reality he was only the man *in* her dreams, not the man *of* her dreams. Was he?

"Thanks for outing me," she grouched, frustrated now by the flip-flop turn of her emotions since he'd called. "Now Lindsay will never leave me alone until I tell her everything that's happened between the two of us since the afternoon we met at Seville's."

"Not everything, I hope." He chuckled and the sound of it coursed over her in waves, making goose flesh rise up on her neck and arms. Shrugging, she rolled her head on her shoulders to ease the sudden flare of heat in those places where she now imagined his warm breath had played a moment before. "Sam, I have to get back to my research. You didn't actually need to call me."

"Sure I did," he insisted. "How else was I to hear your lovely voice this morning? You refused to come by, and I did ask."

"Hm. Well I hope you recorded this conversation for future reference," she snapped saucily, "because the next time you interrupt me for something so silly, I'm going to send the call straight to voice mail."

He laughed. "Are you always a grouch in the mornings?"

Emma made a face at the phone. "Wouldn't you like to know?" she said without thinking, then squeezed her eyes closed in horror because she knew exactly what his next words would be.

"Oh, absolutely. I want to know from personal experience, too. Not some second-hand news. Was that an invitation, Miss Riley?"

Another image flashed through her thoughts, this one of her waking up to Sam leaning over her in her bed, nothing but a sheet draped loosely over his hips, and a smile in his eyes as he kissed her good morning.

Turning around, she searched for Chloe, thinking the cat must be up to some mischief again. Had she somehow managed to drag the quilt into the corner of her living room she'd commandeered for her home office?

"No, and no. That didn't happen," she murmured the last bit mostly to herself in an attempt to keep her dreams and reality straight in her head while bending down sideways to look for Chloe, but Sam still heard her.

"What didn't happen?"

Spotting Chloe on the sofa where she was not supposed to be, Emma remembered she had taken the quilt to Sam's last night. She got up and went to shoo Chloe off the couch and onto the floor.

"You never kissed me good morning," she answered without thinking, then closed her eyes again and groaned in abject mortification. Could this morning possibly get any worse?

"I would have, but again, you refused my invitation, remember? And now you know what you'll be missing every time you turn me down for an early morning meeting at the cafe." He sounded smug. "Good morning kisses are just the beginning, by the way."

Emma couldn't help it. She laughed. She could only imagine what other little treasures Sam was dreaming up to torture her over the loss of even as she scooped Chloe off the sofa. "What do I have to do to get off the phone with you? I've got at least four more hours of work here and morning is about to collide with afternoon, in case you haven't noticed."

"Promise you'll meet me for lunch and I will stop filling your head with thoughts of the two of us embracing at five a. m. in the early morning shadows outside your door."

"Lunch?" Emma complained. "That's barely an hour from now!"

"An hour I will spend every minute of wishing you were here already. I don't think I can wait for you to arrive. As a matter of fact, grab your purse and meet me at the door in fifteen minutes. I'll come and get you," he insisted, and Emma wished she weren't so tempted. She was. To steal away with Sam, to forget responsibility for a little while would be so nice. But it was also the sort of thing she had promised never to do once she'd decided to leave her parents place to make a life for herself.

"Absolutely not. I'm locking my door," she threatened.

His sigh of defeat was loaded with pity-inducing sorrow. "What do I have to do to wring a yes from you, Emma? Show up on your doorstep and kiss you into complacency?"

Oooh, now that was too cruel, making her dream …

"Fine. We will do lunch, Sam. A late one, though." Glancing at her watch, she asked, "Will you still be at the cafe around two?"

She could almost hear the triumphant grin in his voice when he said, "I'll wait for you as long as it takes."

Her lips twisted into a wry grin. "That could be forever. I'm a notorious scatterbrain when I get busy. I bury myself in what I'm doing and tend to forget every-thing else until I'm done."

"Just think about my lips, Emma. On yours. On the soft line of your jaw. Nuzzling up against the sensitive spot on your nape right below your ear," he murmured low, and blast him, she did.

Biting back a groan of yearning, she whispered, "Goodbye, Sam."

She could still hear the sound of his knowing masculine chuckles when she pressed the button to end the call.

CHAPTER EIGHTEEN

The following weeks passed in a magical kind of blur. From the moment she'd joined Sam at the One Shot for "a late lunch," Emma became entrenched—in both the progress of the new construction and redesign of the cafe and in a surprisingly exhilarating and unexpectedly fulfilling, semi-personal relationship with Sam.

The man was perfect. He was beautiful. He was solicitous but not overly adoring. He was quick to ask her opinions and obstinately firm about their importance to him every time she tried to keep them to herself. The One Shot was his cafe and this was his life and her opinions didn't really matter in the overall scheme of things.

Sam was quick to put an end to her hesitance. Her thoughts absolutely mattered, he'd told her more than once, because *she* mattered. And Emma had started to believe him. For whatever reason, he had opened up his life to her, and now she felt as much a part of it as his best friends, Kaylee and Jordan must, as much a part of it as Jabez, the pup he lavished with love and affection, and at least as much a part of it as the coffee shop he loved so much.

Sam had changed her, too, she had to admit, although the realization astounded her. With easy acceptance, he had helped her to open up, to ease past her shyness and to feel confident enough in her own abilities as a smart person with a perfectly functioning mind of her own, to interact with his friends as easily as she did with hers.

Never once in her past had she felt comfortable enough in a relationship with a guy—any guy, even members of her own family—to simply let go and be herself without fear of eventually being shut down and possibly even humiliated, but nothing with Sam was like anything she'd ever experienced before.

Not once in the time she had known him did he seem to look down on her accomplishments. Not once did he belittle her goals or act as if they were unworthy. Sam was the only man she had ever known who looked at her and saw who she really was and didn't try to force her to become someone else. In fact, he wasn't judgmental at all.

As silly as it seemed in this day and age, Sam was the only man who had ever treated her like an equal. He was also the only man who pampered her and spoiled her like a princess. Sometimes when he looked at her, she interpreted his gaze as the same kind of look one might give to a long-coveted treasure finally attained.

He was so sweetly attentive sometimes it made her blush. And yet, at the same time she was secretly thrilled. Deep down she was loving every minute of it … so much she had become a bit wary when they were together lately because she knew all too well how good things eventually came to an end. Especially things that were far too good to be true, and she was a little afraid such was the case with her and Sam.

Any modern-day princess might have looked upon the growing relationship between them with envy, but Emma knew it could come crashing down around her any day, leaving her crushed, broken, and no longer whole.

If she didn't know better, if she hadn't been carefully maintaining a hold on her fragile heart, she might have said they were in love—or at least falling there. The same could not be said, however, for their pets: Chloe and Jabez. Theirs was more a love-hate type thing which changed from one minute to the next, much to both Emma and Sam's amusement.

Their pets antics when they came together were fairly amusing most days … when it wasn't raining out and miserably frigid, like tonight, and when she and Sam weren't forced to go out into the wintry mess to save a madly hissing, furry monster from the clawing branches of a tree in the dark.

Emma had come home with Sam for dinner again, as she had done for two of the past three weeks, and she'd brought Chloe along with her rather than leave her alone for hours at the apartment. Usually, Chloe stayed inside, mostly preferring to sit and stare with disdain at the mortals from her transporter, but somehow tonight, between dinner and dessert, the cat had slipped out of the carrier and wandered outside to inspect the base of a big old Hawthorne tree for suitability as a royal napping place. That was where Jabez had found her and decided to say hello, which was the entire reason Emma was now soaking wet and running for the house with a sopping wet cat in her arms, Sam closing in behind, trying to cover them both with a busted and broken umbrella that wasn't helping at all.

"There's a dish towel in one of the drawers over by the sink." Sam said, sluicing water from his eyes as he pushed open the door and waited for her to go in before following her inside. Scrubbing his muddied boots on the mat, he waved her toward the kitchen. "Go ahead and see to Chloe. I'll find something warm to dry us off."

"And s-something to g-get r-rid of this c-chill!" Emma called through chattering teeth to his retreating back while trying her best to contain the now wriggling, stringy ball of fur in her arms who wanted nothing more at the moment than she wanted down. "C-chloe, you've t-turned into s-such a t-troublemaker, h-haven't you, g-girl?"

After rummaging through a couple drawers, she found a towel and attempted to soak up the water from the cat's soaked and matted fur. "Y-you should b-be ashamed, g-going out into the y-yard like t-that without us. How d-did you g-get out of the c-carrier, anyway?"

"She probably batted at the latch with her paw until it came free," Sam offered as she put a now much less drenched and knotted Chloe on the floor. "Cats are smart like that, I hear."

Casting a glare at the cat, Emma wanted to disagree. But then, Sam draped something fluffy and warm over and around the both of them, cocooning her in warmth before wrapping his arms around her from behind. He pulled her against his chest beneath the toasty warm covering that felt like he'd just pulled it from the dryer and she immediately leaned back to snuggle in closer.

"Mm, there. How's that? This should knock the chill right out of you," he said, nuzzling at her neck even as he snuggled her deeper into his embrace, and without warning or reason, *close* was suddenly not close enough.

Like the thundering jolt of an unexpected electrical current, desire and longing slammed through her, turning her into a quivering, needy mess of unhinged passion Emma neither understood nor tried to deny. Everywhere their bodies touched, she burned. Every spot his breath caressed, she tingled and then, she started to melt against him.

She wanted to wind herself around him, much like Chloe might, kneading his muscles with her fingers while rubbing her body against him at every turn. No. No, she wanted more—needed more than that. She needed to sink *into* him, to be a part of him as he had become a part of everything that was her. The torrential, aching need flooding through her was far too powerful for her to control. There was nothing to be done but give in to it, and so she did.

In that instant, Emma completely forgot about the cold, forgot she was drenched, soaked practically to the bone. She forgot about Chloe and Jabez and the still open kitchen door behind them. In that moment, she forgot everything but Sam. Everything but her suddenly voracious desire and the wickedly delicious feel of his perfectly sculpted hard body pressed against hers.

Turning in his arms, she leaned in until her breasts were flush with his chest, her thighs snug against his, and threaded her fingers into his dripping wet hair. Almost purring with satisfaction from the feel of his scalp beneath her fingertips, her palms, and from the heat of his body pouring into hers, she closed her eyes.

"Oh, Sam. I need you so much," she whispered on a shaky, breathless sigh as her lips sought and found the warm pulse at the base of his throat through the opening at the front of his shirt.

"I want you," she whispered as her fingers left his hair to wander down and up again, this time beneath his soaked shirt, to worship the silky smooth skin of his bare chest. She pushed his shirt upward and he helped her remove it when it became caught on his chin.

Laughing, she tossed it aside, but then grew serious when he slipped his hands beneath the hem of her sweater and then upward.

Leaning into his touch, she murmured her pleasure against his lips, whispering encouragement all the while. Her eyes flew open and her gaze collided with his. He was watching her with an intensity that only sharpened everything she was feeling until her need became almost unbearable.

"Love me," she demanded, pushing her body ever closer to his. "I want you to love me, Sam. *Please*. Love me now, like you did before…"

Sam froze. His fingers gripped her arms and he held onto her even as he pushed her slightly away and shook his head as if to clear thoughts grown as muddled as her own. "Emma? Emma, do you even know what you're saying? You and I, we've never done this before."

Her sultry siren's chuckle should have been his undoing, but still, she followed it with words—a horrible, terrible, damning confession of what had happened between them in her dreams. "Oh, but we have, Sam. We truly have. Every single night for weeks and weeks."

Shrugging off his hands, she wriggled close again and pressed her fingers against the heated contours of his chest before following her questing fingertips with her lips over well-remembered paths.

"Mm," she hummed once in delight before glancing up to meet his confused, questioning gaze. She smiled. "Don't be afraid, Sam. You already know how this is supposed to end. We both do. But if you want to pretend you've grown a little shy…"

Reaching for his hands, she guided them back to the

sagging hem of her damp sweater that hugged the curve of her waist. "Here, let me show you."

A bright flash of light filled the room a split second before a peal of thunder cracked through the night, shaking Emma to her core, and then there was chaos. A streak of white zipped across the room. There was a hiss, and then a crash near the door.

"Arfh! Arfh!"

Jabez.

And Chloe.

Momentarily shaken from the thrall of her desire, Emma turned to go after Chloe but when she did, the black and white checkered quilt Sam had wrapped them in fell away and suddenly Emma knew what had happened.

She recalled every word she had said, every thing she had done, and looking back at Sam, she knew without a doubt that all was lost because after all these weeks she saw at last the judgment she had expected from the beginning in his eyes.

Uncovered now, she could feel the chill of damp cloth seeping into her bones, freezing her from the inside. Wrapping her arms around her middle, she closed her eyes, fighting back tears of shame over what she had done. "I-I'm sorry, Sam. It wasn't really me. Well, it was, but mostly it was whatever came with that quilt, but that's still no excuse for my behavior."

She couldn't look at him again, couldn't wait for him to speak. Spinning on her heel, she made a beeline for

Chloe's transporter, which she grabbed along with her purse from the table beside it and hurried to the door.

Pausing for one quick, last glimpse over her shoulder at the man she now realized she truly had begun to love, she felt lost and alone and afraid. And she was deeply humiliated by how she had acted, what she had done. But worse than either of those was the stabbing pain in the region of her breaking heart because she knew when Sam looked at her now he saw her much differently than before.

Too much passion. Too much enthusiasm. Too much —everything. She'd behaved recklessly. Shamelessly. And in Sam's eyes she could clearly see the appalling truth, the consequences of her actions: she was well and truly condemned.

CHAPTER NINETEEN

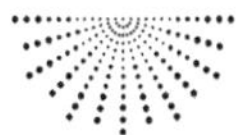

$\mathcal{C}$oming out of a daze he hadn't realized he'd fallen into, Sam blinked once, shook his head, and blinked again. *What in the world had just happened?* Grabbing the quilt now pooled at his feet, he picked it up and tossed it onto the kitchen table. Stumbling toward the door, his still wet boots slipping on the parquet floor, he barely managed to catch Emma before she ran blindly out into the rain again. "Emma, wait."

Shaking her head, she peered into the downpour, one hand coming up to wipe away wetness from her cheek—wetness that made no sense. She hadn't yet stepped off the back stoop but her face was already drenched?

"I have to find Chloe."

There was a thickness in her tone that had him drawing up in shocked realization. The wetness on her face was tears. With a hand on her shoulder, Sam turned her to face him. "You're crying. Why?"

Dashing away the wetness with the back of her hand, she sniffed. "It doesn't matter."

Sam's brows rose so high the thought they must have disappeared into his hairline. "Doesn't matter? You just turned into the most delightful rendition ever of Aprhodite and Eve rolled into one and rather than the moment ending as it should have—with you and me waking up in each other's arms, happy smiles wreathing our faces—you're on the verge of running out into a storm with your vision so impaired by tears you can't see five feet in front of you."

Reaching out, he tilted her chin upward with one hand, forcing her to meet his gaze. "You're hurting, Emma, and that hurts me. Trust me, whatever happened that has you suddenly bursting into tears definitely *matters*—at least to me."

With his thumb, he smoothed away a tear. Searching her eyes, he said, "This isn't like you, Emma. If it's me, if I've done something to hurt you, please tell me."

Her eyes closed and Sam thought he heard her groan. "It isn't *you*, Sam. It's me. Or, rather, it's me anytime I come into contact with that blasted quilt."

Following her accusatory gaze to the coverlet in question, Sam asked, "The quilt? What are you talking about?"

There was indecision in her eyes. "Nothing. It's nothing."

"We've already decided there is definitely more than nothing going on here and I think we need to get to the bottom of this." Catching her hand in his, he reached out with the other to close the door, then tugged her toward the table where he'd tossed the quilt. "What does your kissing me have to do with a wretched bit of bed covering?"

Refusing to look anywhere near the table, Emma said, "I think it's cursed."

Cursed? Sam blinked in confusion, and then understanding dawned. "The quilt! Oh, Kaylee and Jordan are going to love this."

Her eyes widened instantly. "No! You can't, Sam. Don't you dare tell them a thing about how badly I lost control here tonight. I swear, I'll never speak to you again if you do."

"Why not?" He shrugged. "They already know every time I pick up one of those coffee cups or the pot I picked up from Seville's, or if I happen to touch the piece of that wooden puzzle I stole from your box that day, I can't seem to think of anything but you. Why should it matter if they know your enchanted item is the quilt you bought?"

"Enchanted? You're not making sense, Sam. This has nothing to do with magic, but my—" Taking a deep breath, she shrugged and said, "My reckless enthusiasm. My uncontrollable passions and a total lack of good sense required to keep them to myself."

She looked up at him through a watery gaze; her bottom lip trembled, making Sam want to kiss it still again but she had more to say.

"I saw the way you looked at me. I can guess what you

were thinking. My father was right after all. Not being able to exercise even a little bit of restraint over my own emotions ruins everything for me, so just move over and let me collect Chloe so I can go home. I prefer to nurse my wounds in private."

"Now who's not making sense? Emma, what exactly did your father tell you and what does this have to do with you and I?"

Gesturing wildly with her hands, she slashed them through the air, obviously taking out her frustrations on the space in front of her. "He said I was childish, that I tried too hard to make an impression, but as the youngest of five, I've always had to work harder than all my other siblings to get them to notice me. If I hadn't, they might simply have forgotten I existed."

Sam started to tell her what her father had said was ridiculous but he realized at some point in time she had not only come to believe him, she had taken every hurtful word her old man had said to her to heart.

Again, she dashed tears from her cheeks with the back of her hand. "When I told him about my idea for making furniture, he looked down his nose at me, Sam. He gave me the same look you gave me a few moments ago," she accused. "He said I was hopelessly naive and...and reckless. He said I never took the time to think things through, and he was right."

Sam scowled. "Emma—"

"That's the night I left home, Sam. I was nineteen. I sneaked out after dark and hitched a ride to the airport, and called Lindsay to beg her for money for a ticket out here. I left because my father had finally made me realize when I want something I shouldn't just jump in with both feet and hope for the best. I needed to plan, and analyze, and take a little time to think about what I wanted from life because most of the time, if I'd given any one of my hair-brained schemes a little consideration, the facts I found would easily have shown me I was wasting my time."

Crossing his arms over his chest, Sam guessed, "That's why you became a research specialist. You needed to work in facts?"

"I had to show him he was wrong about me, Sam. I could make careful, measured, grown-up decisions as well as either of my brothers. I had to prove to him that I wasn't the feather-brained, recklessly abandoned, naive little girl he thought me to be."

"Your *father* is the reason you shut down?" Sam muttered darkly. "I wondered who was responsible, but I thought it would be someone else—an old love, maybe. But... your father?"

Shaking his head, he pinned her with a look. "You're still giving him control, aren't you? Even after he made you close yourself off from the world, shut up your creativity and your genius and even your desire to live life on your own terms."

"Grandma Ellie always told me every person is born with the power to change the world inside them. All they need do is be brave enough to set it free—and you tried.

But then you let him get to you. You locked yourself away inside your own little world where you somehow managed to convince yourself you weren't worthy of consideration—by anyone. That *your* thoughts and ideas weren't important. That *your* wants, needs, and desires didn't matter..."

Anger rose up inside of him at the thought of a scared young girl alone in the world desperately trying to make a name from herself with a total lack of support from anyone just to win the love and approval of a man who, in his opinion, didn't deserve anything from her. "You should be proud, Emma."

Looking up at him with wounded eyes from beneath her lashes, she asked, "Proud? But I've just proved everything he ever told me was right! I let my emotions overrule my head, Sam, at the most important juncture of my life. I've made a fool of myself with you, over you, and now..."

"No," he insisted quietly. "You are perfect to me, Emma. Can't you see that?"

Closing the three steps that separated them, he placed his palms on both sides of her face and lifted it until she could see the truth in his eyes. "Your spontaneity, your quick thinking, your passion and enthusiasm—those are all things I *love* about you."

When she started to protest, he continued. "Look at what they have brought you, look at all they have helped you accomplish since the day you decided to go to

Seville's for a little extra credit research into puzzles for your client."

She scowled. "That cursed quilt?"

Sam laughed. "It was what caught my attention and drew it to you, so I wouldn't call it cursed at all. But that isn't what I meant, Emma. Since the day you walked into Seville's, your life immediately began to change—for the better. In a few short weeks, aside from proving yourself as a competent research specialist, you've become a business consultant, an architectural design assistant, and even a published author."

Peering into her eyes, he said, "Now tell me you could have accomplished all that in such a short time frame if you had been careful with your ideas? If you'd bottled up your impulses like you say your father insisted you should. Emma, if you hadn't allowed your curiosity about the coffee service to lure you into doing some unpaid but meticulously thorough research, if you'd waited until you knew the facts about my business before you drew up what you imagined when you looked out the back windows of the OneShot ... "

Drawing her close, he finished with, "What would have happened to us if you hadn't let your impulses convince you to buy that quilt and then dreamed of me so often that when we came together outside your subconscious you felt like you knew me already?"

Her brows drew together. "You knew about the dreams?"

"I did. But I had no clue how powerful a wallop the

sisters packed into that quilt until you kissed me like you did the night at the One Shot and then asked me to love you like I had *before*," he teased. "I think I even felt a little cheated because I had no memory of loving you the way you clearly remembered it."

Emma's cheeks flushed bright and she buried her face against his chest. "Don't. Oh, God, don't remind me. I think I want to crawl way up into the back of Chloe's transporter now and hide."

"Why?" There was laughter in his voice when he assured her, "Your kisses are spectacular, Emma. Trust me, darling, you've done nothing to be ashamed of."

"Are you saying you aren't appalled by my reckless, passionate abandon? You—you really don't want me to leave?"

Tenderly, Sam cupped her cheek in the palm of one hand. The other, he held up in front of her, the puzzle piece he'd filched from her the day they'd met at Seville's between his finger and thumb. "This is you, Emma. You're the piece that has been missing from the puzzle of my life. Without you, I will always be missing something —a piece of my heart, of myself. If you leave me, I will never be whole again."

"Oh, Sam." Her lips were quivering again, he noticed, and her eyes had once again sprung a leak. "That was beautiful."

He brushed a curl from her forehead and leaned in for a kiss. "*You* are beautiful, Emma Riley. You are beautiful and perfect in all the ways that matter, and that is why to the depths of my soul, I absolutely love you."

He felt it when her fingers threaded their way into his hair. Felt it when she finally let go of the pain of her past. When she pressed her lips to his and when she finally set herself free. "I love you, too, Sam Huntingdon the Third. I think I've loved you from the moment I first saw you when you walked into the showroom of Seville's."

Sam couldn't have repressed the devilish twinkle in his eyes if he'd tried when he took her hands in his and said, "Show me."

CHAPTER TWENTY

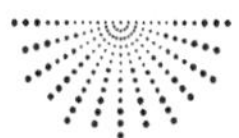

lthough it seemed the entire populous of Hawthorne Grove turned out for the grand re-opening of the One Shot Coffee Cafe, Emma was surprisingly calm. Lindsay would have said it was the costume that kept her settled. Dressed from feet to feathered headdress in an outfit straight out of a Victorian fashion catalog, she looked like a high-born lady of old. But Emma knew her serenity today had nothing to do with what she was wearing, but rather, the handsome gentleman at her side, also rocking full Victorian dress.

Everyone fully expected to see their host smiling and chatting with his loyal customers while he assisted the baristas, handing out steaming mugs filled with piping hot coffee but for once, Sam was not holding court behind the bar. Instead, he stood beside her at the door, greeting customers before handing them off to Lindsay for the first stage of the re-opening tour.

Sam had decided to turn the re-opening into an event to remember and it began with meeting Emma at the entrance. He'd had Lindsay set up a special table for her and she sat there now, stacks of her book waiting in front of her, which she was happy to sign for anyone who asked...and most did, too her surprise.

But Emma wasn't surprised in the least to discover Sam knew most of the people who came in by their first names. He'd say hello, thank them for coming in, then introduce them to Emma—his fiance—and then he would escort each group over to Lindsay for an introduction because the One Shot's stunning new interior was every inch her baby.

Lindsay Vale of *Vale's Vintage Interiors* was an amazing woman, it turned out, who had a flair for all things vintage. From the curtains now draping the tall windows to the soft lamps gracing the antiqued tables, to the authentic period seating, Lindsay was responsible for it all.

Mauve and lavender chairs, rose and cream settees, and even the delicate, vibrant spring green vine borders that were replicated from the wallpaper into the drapes turned the main room of Sam's coffee cafe into the epitome of a stately Victorian parlor. The place was the perfect reproduction of an actual parlor from centuries ago—an exquisite, untouched piece of history brought forward in time for the enjoyment of all.

The women, Emma noticed, absolutely loved the main room, but Sam had put in both a vintage card room and two very manly studies off the main room for the men who wanted their coffee but could do without the more feminine frippery. And there were the florists, of course, up on the second floor.

Lindsay had convinced Sam to bring Rowena's Nightshades – Hawthorne Grove's infamous "after hours florist" into the building early on, but she had also put him in touch with Melissa Sutton, another florist from out of town who could use the boost in foot traffic, who'd set up Morning Glory—a flower shop that was open during daylight hours on one half of the top floor—while Rowena's after-dark only floral specialty shop occupied the other.

From her chair near the door, Emma watched the milling crowd with pride, happy to see such a turn out for Sam's special day. His regular customers and even a few new ones had moved off to sit at the various tables strategically placed around the main room. All of them sipped their favorite java brew from a mix of earthenware and delicate china cups. Women *ooohed* and *aaaahed* over the newly redecorated interior and men shared hearty back-slaps of relief over Sam's thoughtfulness in creating a few rooms just for the men.

Kaylee's older sister and Sam's best customer, Jo Dean Leavy, who was also regaled in full Victorian dress, sat at a special table on the other side of the *chiffonier* Jordan had restored for the occasion, reading aloud from her own signed copy of Emma's book: *Did Queens Drink Coffee? And Other Interesting Facts About Your Favorite Bean.*

Emma knew it was Jo's excellent reading voice that drew people to her table like a magnet. Eventually everyone who came in wandered over to hear and to see the antique coffee service that had once belonged to a queen, but Sam insisted it was Emma's fine writing that kept them enthralled. She had sold over an hundred copies of her book—and that was just since this morning!

As delighted as she was for Sam's success, by lunchtime, Emma was tired of sitting in one place. Her back ached from the corset she was wearing for the occasion and her cheeks hurt from all the non-stop smiling she was doing. It was time for a break.

Pushing her chair back from the table, she got to her feet and said, "I have to move around for a while, Sam. This blasted corset is killing me. Can we show them the rest now?"

"You just want to curl up away from the lunch crowd under our quilt in the Latte Lounge, don't you?" he teased, but like a true gentleman, he took her hand and placed it in the crook of his arm, motioning across the room to Jordan to open the double doors leading out onto the back terrace.

Leading the way, Sam motioned to a few people, indicating they should follow him, calling over his shoulder as he went. "And now, ladies and gentlemen, if you will follow me ... the *piece de resistance!*"

Strolling arm in arm along a newly laid, winding cobblestone lane that meandered from the terrace to the coffee cottages, Sam and Emma led the way to what looked like a tiny Victorian village among the trees at the back of the cafe. He stopped in front of one of the buildings and held up a hand. "Welcome to Cozy Lane, where you can have your java beverage of choice and a bit more privacy for doing those things you love while you drink: surf the 'Net, read a book, the paper, or just enjoy the peace and quiet of fifteen minutes of downtime with a tasty aromatic blend in your cup the next time you stop by the One Shot for a cuppa Joe."

~

AT THE EDGE OF TOWN, Serephina Seville watched the goings on in the mercury waters filling the sisters' scrying dish with relief. "Well, it looks like we did it, Morty. Sam proposed, Emma accepted and they both look so happy together."

"Yep!" Mortianna agreed. Unfurling herself from the sofa, she said, "But I'm still a bit worried about Sam's easy acceptance of the idea of that quilt being magically influenced."

"It will fade," Serephina assured her. "People tend to forget about the inexplicable unless it keeps showing up in their lives and you know that isn't how we work."

"Kaylee and Jordan didn't forget," Mortianna reminded her sister. "What are we going to do if people start spreading it around that Seville's is the place to go if you want to find the love of your life?"

"No more than we do now, Morty. If we get

customers, there will be an item with our number on it to sell to them and we will sell it. Simple as that."

"Hm. Only it's not. You're forgetting about the bracelet. There were no numbers on that, or on the handful of charms we sold that engineer guy." Her expression turned curious. "You knew there were no numbers, too, didn't you? Why did you sell them to him, anyway?"

Serephina waved away her concerns. "Will you stop trying to borrow trouble, Morty? We have enough as it is, or had you forgotten about Merry's extended absence?"

"Not for a minute. How long do you think it will take for the CHG to release her, now that our couple is happy?"

"I'm not sure they will, Mortianna." Serephina frowned. "That quilt wasn't meant to go to Emma Riley and the puzzle …"

Mortianna shook her head in denial. "That quilt was *exactly* what Emma needed to bring her out of her self-constructed shell and you know it. And the puzzle is no different than those charms. Sam thought of Emma every time he touched or thought of that thing and there wasn't a bit of magic in it yet. Unless you know something I don't?"

Ignoring the niggling feeling that there was more than a little truth in what her sister had said, Serephina shook her head to deny it, and Morty shrugged and pasted a happy grin over an equally fake positive expression. "Maybe you just misunderstood the orders."

Or maybe there was something else at work when that quilt got handed off to the wrong woman, Serephina thought, but she didn't mention it to Mortianna. "Put the dish away for me, will you, Morty? And meet me in the shop when you're done. There's something I want to show you."

Mortianna's eyes widened. "Oooh! Feeny, did we get a new item to sell?"

"Something like that," Serephina hedged, clasping her hands together in front of her to keep from wringing them. "It has our numbers on it anyway."

"Our numbers, but no order?" Mortianna made a face. "We'd better leave it alone then, until we get some instruction from the higher ups. I don't think we can handle another screw up and subsequent disappearance like this one with Merry."

Casting her sister a look, Serephina shrugged and turned to leave. "Suit yourself, Mortianna, but it was delivered here this morning with a note from your favorite Keeper."

And it was the note more than the numbered item she had received that bothered Serephina, although she would not mention the cryptic message to her sister. Not here. Not yet. Instead, she made for the stairs, knowing Mortianna's curiosity would have her following soon enough.

While she waited? She would read the note again

because she was sure there was something terribly important hidden in the message Airrick Skurlock had sent to them this morning ... and it concerned Mortianna.

****

Sign up for my VIP reader list and get my books at the lowest discount price:
http://www.leighanndobbs.com/leighann-dobbs-romance-email-list/

Join my Facebook Readers group and get special content and the inside scoop on my books:
https://www.facebook.com/groups/ldobbsreaders

More Books in the Hawthorne Grove Series:
Something Magical (Book 1)

If you want to receive a text message on your cell phone for new releases, text ROMANCE to 88202 (sorry, this only works for US cell phones!)

ALSO BY LEIGHANN DOBBS

Contemporary Romance

***

Reluctant Romance

Silver Hollow

Paranormal Romance / Cozy Mystery Series

***

A Spell of Trouble (Book 1)

Spell Disaster (Book 2)

Nothing to Croak About (Book 3)

Sweet Romance (Written As Annie Dobbs)

Hometown Hearts Series

***

No Getting Over You (Book 1)

Magical Romance with a Touch of Mystery

***

Something Magical

Cozy Mysteries

Mystic Notch

Cat Cozy Mystery Series

* * *

Ghostly Paws

A Spirited Tail

A Mew To A Kill

Paws and Effect

Probable Paws

Blackmoore Sisters

Cozy Mystery Series

* * *

Dead Wrong

Dead & Buried

Dead Tide

Buried Secrets

Deadly Intentions

A Grave Mistake

Spell Found

Mooseamuck Island Cozy Mystery Series

* * *

A Zen For Murder

A Crabby Killer

A Treacherous Treasure

Lexy Baker Cozy Mystery Series

* * *

Lexy Baker Cozy Mystery Series Boxed Set Vol 1 (Books 1-4)

Or buy the books separately:

Killer Cupcakes

Dying For Danish

Murder, Money and Marzipan

3 Bodies and a Biscotti

Brownies, Bodies & Bad Guys

Bake, Battle & Roll

Wedded Blintz

Scones, Skulls & Scams

Ice Cream Murder

Mummified Meringues

Brutal Brulee (Novella)

No Scone Unturned

***

Sweetrock Sweet and Spicy Cowboy Romance

Some Like It Hot

Too Close For Comfort

————

Regency Romance

* * *

Scandals and Spies Series:

Kissing The Enemy

The Unexpected Series:

An Unexpected Proposal

Dobbs Fancytales:

Dobbs Fancytales Boxed Set Collection

————

Western Historical Romance

***

Goldwater Creek Mail Order Brides:

Faith

American Mail Order Brides Series:

Chevonne: Bride of Oklahoma

———————————————

USA Today Bestselling author Leighann Dobbs has had a passion for reading since she was old enough to hold a book, but she didn't put pen to paper until much later in life. After a twenty-year career as a software engineer with a few side trips into selling antiques and making jewelry, she realized you can't make a living reading books, so she tried her hand at writing them and discovered she had a passion for that, too! She lives in New Hampshire with her husband, Bruce, their trusty Chihuahua mix, Mojo, and beautiful rescue cat, Kitty.

Her book "Dead Wrong" won the "Best Mystery Romance" award at the 2014 Indie Romance Convention.

Her book "Ghostly Paws" was the 2015 Chanticleer Mystery & Mayhem First Place category winner in the Animal Mystery category.

Don't miss out on the early buyers discount on Leighann's next cozy mystery - signup for email notifications:

http://www.leighanndobbs.com/leighann-dobbs-romance-email-list/

Want text alerts for new releases? TEXT alert straight on your cellphone. Just text ROMANCE to 88202
(sorry, this only works for US cell phones!)

Connect with Leighann on Facebook:
http://facebook.com/leighanndobbsbooks

Join her VIP Readers group on Facebook:
https://www.facebook.com/groups/ldobbsreaders

∼

This is a work of fiction.

None of it is real. All names, places, and events are products of the author's imagination. Any resemblance to real names, places, or events are purely coincidental, and should not be construed as being real.

CURIOUSLY ENCHANTED

Copyright © 2017

Leighann Dobbs Publishing

http://www.leighanndobbs.com

All Rights Reserved.

No part of this work may be used or reproduced in any manner, except as allowable under "fair use," without the express written permission of the author.

www.ingramcontent.com/pod-product-compliance
Lightning Source LLC
Chambersburg PA
CBHW070941190726
48292CB00004B/1285